THE ELUSIVE HEIRESS

NANCY DREW MYSTERY STORIES®

THE ELUSIVE HEIRESS

by
Carolyn Keene

Illustrated by
Paul Frame

WANDERER BOOKS

Published by Simon & Schuster, New York

Published by WANDERER BOOKS
A Simon & Schuster Division of
Gulf & Western Corporation
Simon & Schuster Building
1230 Avenue of the Americas
New York, New York 10020

Manufactured in the United States of America
10 9 8 7 6 5 4 3 2 1

NANCY DREW and NANCY DREW MYSTERY STORIES
are trademarks of Stratemeyer Syndicate,
registered in the United States Patent
and Trademark Office

WANDERER and colophon are trademarks of Simon & Schuster

Library of Congress Cataloging in Publication Data

Keene, Carolyn.
The elusive heiress.

(Nancy Drew mystery stories; 68)
Summary: Nancy's search for the long-missing daughter of an
aging millionaire takes her to Cheyenne, Wyoming, during its
annual Frontier Days celebration.
[1. Mystery and detective stories. 2. Wyoming—
Fiction] I. Frame, Paul, 1913-   ill. II. Title.
III. Series: Keene, Carolyn. Nancy Drew mystery
stories; 68.
PZ7.K23   Nan no. 68   [Fic]   81-19805
ISBN 0-671-44555-3   AACR2
ISBN 0-671-44553-7 (pbk.)

Contents

Contents

1

Anxious Search

"I think I have a case that will interest you, Nancy," Carson Drew told his titian-haired daughter as he handed her a cool glass of lemonade. "It has to do with Arlo Winthrop."

"The millionaire?" Nancy sipped the lemonade and reached for one of the cookies Hannah Gruen had placed on the picnic table in the backyard of their River Heights home.

Her father nodded, sitting down beside her. "Mr. Winthrop has been in poor health for some time and now he's very anxious to set his affairs in order. To do that, he would like to know once and for all what happened to his daughter Clarinda."

"I didn't know he had a daughter," Nancy commented, her curiosity immediately caught. "I know his nephew has lived in the mansion with him for years—ever since Mr. Winthrop's son died, but . . ."

"Clarinda Winthrop left home forty years ago when she was just eighteen. She and her father quarreled because he wished her to marry a young man he considered a suitable match and she claimed to be in love with a young soldier she'd met at a friend's house. Her father disinherited her at the time, but in the past few years, he's had Tom Mathews order several searches for her."

"Is Tom Mathews his nephew?" Nancy asked.

Her father nodded. "They've traced her as far as Cheyenne, Wyoming. That is where her soldier was from." He paused and took several old snapshots from his pocket and handed them to Nancy. "That is Clarinda."

Nancy stared at the pretty young face framed by a cloud of dark hair done in a neat pageboy. The brown eyes were serious even though the girl was smiling at the camera. "She looks so young," Nancy commented, sure that the girl couldn't be any older than she was.

"Barely eighteen," her father confirmed.

"And her father hasn't heard anything from her in all the years since?"

"I talked with Tom Mathews and looked over the reports from the private investigators that he hired and they didn't seem to be able to find out what happened to her after she reached Cheyenne. Of course, Mr. Winthrop didn't start the searches until she'd been gone over thirty years, so it isn't surprising they had difficulties."

Nancy frowned, though her blue eyes were sparkling at the challenge. "What makes you think we can do better, Dad?" she asked.

"We have a secret weapon," he informed her with a grin. "Remember Grace Reed?"

"Of course," Nancy agreed. "She's an old friend of Mother's from before you and she were married." Nancy had heard many stories from her father about the happy days when her mother and Grace had been best friends. "I forgot that she lives in Cheyenne," she admitted.

"I called her from the office after I finished talking to Mr. Winthrop, and she has invited us to be her guests for as long as the investigation takes," her father went on, his twinkling gaze

9

telling her that there was more to the story. "And it is just as well she offered us a place to stay."

"Why is that, Dad?" Nancy asked.

"Because there isn't a hotel or motel room to be had in Cheyenne and there won't be for over a week. This Friday marks the first day of the big rodeo there—Cheyenne Frontier Days."

"How exciting," Nancy exclaimed. "I've heard a lot about the rodeo. Do you think we'll have time to see some of the events?"

Her father laughed. "Grace would never forgive us if we didn't," he told her. "Now, do you think you'd be interested in this little mystery?"

Nancy giggled, well aware that he was teasing. "Do you really have to ask?" she replied, then sobered as her attention returned to the girl in the pictures she still held. "I'd really like to help find her," she said. "She looks like some one I could enjoy knowing."

Her father's smile was gentle. "That picture was taken forty years ago," he reminded her. "She may very well be a grandmother by now."

Nancy gave him a solemn stare. "I like grandmothers, too."

They laughed together easily, then Carson explained the travel arrangements he'd made, ending, "I know it is short notice, but do you think you could be packed and ready by early tomorrow morning?"

Nancy swallowed hard, then nodded. "If Hannah is willing to help and I start right now."

Her father leaned back in his chair. "She should be through with my packing by now, so you run along. We can talk more about the case tonight. Mr. Mathews promised to have copies made of the detective reports, so they should be arriving pretty soon. I know you'll want to read them over, too."

"Oh, Dad, I have a date with Ned this evening." Nancy stopped at the door that led to the kitchen. "Do you think I should call him and cancel?" Reluctance showed in her voice as she mentioned the handsome young man she'd been dating.

Her father's eyes met hers for a moment, then he waved a hand. "No reason to cancel. You'll have plenty of time to get caught up on all the details of the case on our flight to Cheyenne. Just don't be late tonight. We have to leave early, you know."

"We're just going to a movie downtown," Nancy replied. "We'll come back here afterward. I'm sure Ned will be interested in the details of such a strange case."

Though the movie was an exciting and entertaining one, all too often Nancy found her mind wandering from the plot. She kept thinking about the girl in the old snapshots.

Where could she have gone? Had something happened to her Wyoming soldier? And if he hadn't returned to her, what could have become of her?

"I envy you flying off to the rodeo," Ned said as he drove her home from the movie. "I've heard so much about all the activities that go on in Cheyenne. I expect you'll have time to enjoy some of them, won't you?"

"Dad seems to think so," Nancy answered, wishing that she could ask Ned to join them, but aware that she couldn't, since they were to be Grace Reed's guests. "Of course, it depends on what we find out about Clarinda once we get to Cheyenne. If we discover that she left there, we may not be staying very long."

"That would be a shame."

"Will you come in for a while?" Nancy invited as he parked in front of her house. "I'm sure Hannah has baked some brownies and Dad may have learned something more about the case."

"I'll stay as long as you'll let me," Ned told her with a smile. "After all, you're leaving tomorrow and you could be gone quite a while."

"I don't . . ." Nancy began, but before she could continue, the porch light flashed on and the front door opened.

"I'm glad you're home," her father called, his forehead furrowed with a frown.

"Is something wrong, Dad?" Nancy asked. "What has happened?"

"Well, I think we may have a problem," her father replied. "Come on inside and I'll explain while we have some of Hannah's brownies and milk."

"So what happened?" Nancy asked once they were settled at the table.

"I got a mysterious phone call a little while ago," Carson began.

"From whom?" Nancy asked.

He shrugged. "It was a woman's voice, but she wouldn't identify herself. However, she did

14

mention an interesting name—Clarinda Winthrop."

"Was it her?" Nancy gasped.

"I don't know," he admitted. "I suppose it could have been."

"So, what did she say?" Nancy asked.

"That I should come to Chain Creek Lodge if I wanted to learn the truth about Clarinda Winthrop."

"Chain Creek Lodge?" Ned said. "Where is that?"

"Somewhere in western Canada, not too far from Calgary, Alberta, according to the map." Carson Drew didn't sound happy.

"Are we going there?" Nancy inquired.

Her father sighed, then shook his head. "Not we—I'm going. I think you should go ahead with our original plan. This could just be a false lead. When someone calls and refuses to give me her name, I have to wonder why."

"You mean you want me to go to Cheyenne alone?" Nancy asked, not liking the idea at áll.

"Well, actually, I've been thinking about that and I wondered if Ned would like to go." Her father turned his attention to the dark-haired young man sitting beside her. "I realize it is

15

short notice, but I talked to Grace and she said that she'd be happy to have you as her guest, too, Ned, if you're free to go."

"Well, I don't . . ." Ned began, surprise showing in his brown eyes.

"I'm sure you can work something out, can't you?" Nancy teased, remembering the longing in his voice when they'd talked about her trip earlier.

"I really don't like the idea of Nancy traveling so far alone," Carson continued. "And, of course, I should be able to join you in a day or two. Unless my mysterious caller actually was Clarinda Winthrop."

"I don't know whether to hope it was her or it wasn't," Nancy said, her blue eyes dancing. "I know it's important that we find her quickly, but I really was looking forward to working out the riddle of her disappearance while I was enjoying Rodeo Week."

Both her father and Ned laughed indulgently. "You just don't want anyone else solving your mystery," her father teased.

"Well, are you going to help me, Ned?" Nancy asked.

His grin was wide and very attractive as he

nodded his head. "I'll have to make a few phone calls and do some packing, but I think I can work it out and I would love to make the trip."

Nancy picked up her milk glass in a toast and the others joined her. "To our successful hunt for Clarinda Winthrop." Smiling, they sipped from their glasses and began making plans for the two separate journeys.

2

Young Traveler

The airport was busy and crowded and Nancy
was glad of Ned's company as they hurried to
the correct boarding area. Since her father's
plane had left a short time before theirs, there
was no one to bid them good-bye.

"Nancy Drew?" The voice was unfamiliar
and Nancy turned slowly to see a very worried-
looking middle-aged lady standing in the line
behind them. "You are Nancy Drew, aren't
you?" the woman asked rather shyly.

Nancy nodded politely, none too comfortable
with the fame she'd gained from solving mysteries. "I'm afraid I don't know who you are,"
she admitted.

"Oh, you wouldn't know me," the woman said quickly. "I'm Mrs. Peterson from De-Cateur Academy, the girls' school."

"I've heard of it," Nancy said, noticing for the first time that the woman was accompanied by a very pretty little blond girl who appeared to be about ten years old.

"I wouldn't bother you," Mrs. Peterson went on, "except that I was wondering if you were going to be on this flight?"

Nancy hesitated a moment, then decided that the woman seemed genuinely upset about something. "I'm flying to Cheyenne, Wyoming," she admitted.

The woman's frown was immediately replaced by a relieved smile. "Oh, that's wonderful, Miss Drew," Mrs. Peterson said, then turned her attention to the girl beside her. "Did you hear that, Jennifer?" she asked. "Miss Drew is going to Cheyenne, too."

Brown eyes looked at Nancy appraisingly and when Nancy smiled at her, Jennifer smiled back shyly, though she didn't say anything. Nancy returned her attention to the woman.

"Jennifer has to make the trip alone," Mrs. Peterson went on. "It's a family emergency and

19

there's no one to fly with her, so I was wondering . . ." She began to look uncomfortable. "I know it is presumptuous of me, Miss Drew, but I'd feel so much better if I knew that you would keep an eye on Jennifer, see that she makes the proper plane changes, things like that. I was going to ask the flight attendants, but they can get so busy. . . ." The woman let it trail off, her expression so full of hopefulness Nancy wanted to pat her shoulder reassuringly.

"I'd be happy to have Jennifer's company," she assured the woman, then turned her attention to the little girl. "Is someone meeting you in Cheyenne, Jennifer?" she asked.

"My mother," Jennifer responded softly.

Mrs. Peterson nodded. "Lorna Buckman," she confirmed. "She called and said that she would meet Jennifer in Cheyenne."

Nancy introduced Ned to Jennifer and Mrs. Peterson, then the line moved and other matters claimed her attention. Before she knew it, they were on the plane and ready to take off for the long, cross-country flight.

It was an uneventful trip. Jennifer proved to be a good traveling companion, spending much of her time looking out the window at the clouds below them or reading the books and magazines Mrs. Peterson had given her before she said good-bye at the gate. She also had a rather elaborate board game that she taught Ned to play while Nancy took time to read the detective reports her father had given her before she left.

"I'm glad Jennifer came with us," Ned teased when Nancy stopped her reading to enjoy lunch. "Otherwise I wouldn't have had anyone to talk to."

Jennifer smiled up at him. "I'm glad you're going to Cheyenne," she said. "Maybe you can come and have dinner with us, if Mom is well enough."

"Has your mother been ill?" Nancy asked, suddenly realizing that it was a little strange for a child Jennifer's age to be in school so far from home.

Jennifer nodded, her eyes darkening. "She was in a car accident and had to stay in the hospital. That's why I went to boarding school. I was supposed to stay the rest of the summer, but Mom must be better, 'cause she said I should come home."

"Are you looking forward to the big rodeo?" Ned asked.

Jennifer nodded. "Last year, I rode in one of

the parades. I was in a Pony Club then."

"Did you like boarding school?" Nancy inquired.

"Mrs. Peterson is nice," Jennifer responded. "She is our housemother. But it was more fun last winter, when everyone was staying at school. There were only a dozen of us there for the summer. Of course, we had the horses to ride and we didn't have any school work, but. . . ." She let it trail off, brushing back her long, straight blond hair. "It will be better with Mom."

Nancy smiled at her. "I'm sure it will," she agreed. "And I bet she's very anxious to see you, too."

It was late afternoon when the plane circled and dropped down to the airport at Cheyenne, Wyoming, and Nancy was happy to gather her papers and belongings to get off. Though Ned and Jennifer had provided pleasant company, the reports had merely whetted her appetite for solving the mystery of what had happened to Clarinda Winthrop.

According to what the detectives had found in both of their investigations, Clarinda Winthrop had taken a train west, arriving in

Cheyenne about two weeks after she disappeared from her father's home. Once in Cheyenne, she'd taken a room in a boardinghouse and was rumored to have found a job in a local dry goods store.

Much checking, however, had not turned up any records of her residence or employment. In fact, it seemed that no one named Clarinda Winthrop had left a single trace in Cheyenne's many records. The two agencies had also tried to locate her in Denver and even checked a few more-distant cities, but they had found nothing.

"Are we being met, too, Nancy?" Ned asked, breaking into her thoughts.

Nancy looked around quickly, blushing slightly, then waved. "Mrs. Reed," she called, easily recognizing their hostess's round figure and warm smile. "Over here!"

Grace Reed hurried to give Nancy a hug, then stepped away from her. "Don't you look more like your mother every day?" she said. "And so grown up, too."

"And you don't get a day older," Nancy informed her, then quickly introduced Ned and Jennifer, adding, "Jennifer's mother is supposed to be here to meet her."

Mrs. Reed smiled at the little girl, who was looking around rather nervously. "She's probably still stuck in traffic outside," she soothed her. "Seems like half of Cheyenne was coming out to meet someone today."

"Why don't we see about the luggage, Jennifer?" Ned suggested. "You can show me which ones are yours, all right?"

Nancy gave him a grateful smile as he took the little girl over to where the luggage was being unloaded. Once Jennifer was gone, she allowed a little frown to touch her normally smooth forehead. "I can't imagine where her mother is," she told Mrs. Reed. "Mrs. Peterson assured me that she'd be meeting Jennifer."

"Mrs. Peterson?"

Nancy quickly explained how she and Ned had come to have Jennifer's company for the flight and also told the attractive, gray-haired widow the few facts she'd learned from Jennifer's conversation. Mrs. Reed shook her head as Nancy finished.

"That's an awfully long flight for a child that age to have to take alone," she commented. "She was lucky to have you and your young man to watch over her."

Nancy blushed a little at the description of Ned and hastily informed Mrs. Reed that Jennifer had entertained Ned for her while she worked on the mystery she'd come to solve. "It's as though Clarinda Winthrop just vanished from the face of the earth," she finished. "I'm not sure where we can begin."

"Well, I have some names for you, Nancy," Mrs. Reed told her, "old timers who might be able to tell you about her. Carson told me that she might have worked for a dry goods store and I know Webber's was the biggest store here at that time. Anyway, Joshua Webber is still living, so he might be able to give you some idea of what happened to her if she worked for him."

"Oh, that would be a wonderful place to begin," Nancy agreed, her spirits lifting after the discouraging reports she'd read. Before she could go on, however, Ned and Jennifer came back to join them and she could see that Jennifer was looking very worried.

"No sign of your mother?" Nancy asked.

The blond head shook emphatically.

"Why don't I go talk to some of the counter people?" Mrs. Reed volunteered. "Maybe Mrs. Buckman has been delayed and called in a message. It's been so noisy and crowded, we wouldn't have heard a page."

"Maybe we could call your mother, Jennifer," Nancy suggested, looking around at the emptying airport. "Do you know your phone number?"

"I don't remember," Jennifer admitted nervously.

"We'll look in the telephone book or call information," Nancy told her, taking her hand as they went to the bank of telephones.

Ten minutes later, she and Jennifer rejoined Ned and Mrs. Reed. "Any luck?" Ned asked.

Nancy sighed. "Her phone has been disconnected and there is no new listing." Nancy looked hopefully toward Mrs. Reed.

The older woman shook her head. Jennifer burst into tears.

"It will be all right," Nancy assured her, dropping to her knees beside the child. "We'll find your mother, I promise."

"Nancy is a very good detective," Mrs. Reed agreed, adding her soothing voice to Nancy's assurances. "And in the meantime, we'll all go to my house. You can stay with me, Jennifer, till we find your mother. Would you like that?"

The sobs slowed a little as Jennifer looked at Nancy. "Will you really find her for me?" she asked.

"I'll do my very best," Nancy answered, sure that it would be much easier to find a woman who'd only been missing one day than to locate one who had disappeared forty years ago.

As they left the airport, Nancy cast one last glance around, her attention caught by a prickly feeling of being watched. Two young men she'd noticed before were now standing near the telephones and she felt their eyes following them as they crossed the room with Jennifer.

27

3

Vanished!

Mrs. Reed's home was a handsome, two-story brick located just on the edge of the city and Nancy could see that the warm, friendly greeting of Mrs. Reed's big collie helped Jennifer to feel better.

"Why don't you and Brewster go and explore the backyard?" Mrs. Reed suggested to the little girl. "His ball is out there somewhere and he dearly loves to chase it. I'm afraid I've been so busy getting ready for Frontier Days, I've been neglecting him."

Once Jennifer was out of earshot, Nancy turned to her hostess. "What do you think I should do, Mrs. Reed?" she asked. "Should I call Mrs. Peterson?"

"I think so. But why don't you call me Grace? Mrs. Reed is much too formal, since we're all going to be living here together."

Nancy smiled. "Thank you, Grace," she said, excusing herself to the telephone, which sat on a small table in one corner of the room. Her conversation with Mrs. Peterson lasted several minutes, but when it finally ended, Nancy hung up with a long sigh.

"What'd she say?" Ned asked when Nancy joined him and Mrs. Reed again.

"Just that there have been no messages from Jennifer's mother since we left River Heights. Mrs. Peterson is terribly upset about everything, and she apologized profusely for any inconvenience she may have caused us—"

"Nonsense," Mrs. Reed said, "and I hope you assured her not to worry."

"Oh, I did," Nancy replied.

"Now, why don't I call the police?" the woman suggested.

"It's really very kind of you to get involved like this." Nancy sighed. "I just never dreamed

29

that her mother wouldn't be waiting for her. Mrs. Peterson seemed so sure."

"Jennifer didn't." Ned broke into the conversation for the first time.

"What do you mean?" Nancy asked, surprised.

"Well, we were talking while you were reading and apparently Jennifer never spoke to her mother when she called for her to come home. She was a little hurt to think that her mother didn't even want to talk to her."

"That is strange," Nancy observed. "Do you suppose it could have been some terrible practical joke?"

"Surely Mrs. Peterson wouldn't have been fooled," Ned said. "She seemed like a very conscientious housemother to Jennifer."

"That's true," Nancy agreed, but her thoughts strayed for a moment to the two young men she'd noticed at the airport. They had certainly seemed interested in Jennifer. But if they'd been sent by her mother, why hadn't they approached the girl? It was really very confusing.

"I'll call the police," Mrs. Reed repeated forcefully, heading for the telephone. "Meantime, Nancy, why don't you pour some lemonade for us? And there are fresh-baked cookies in the ceramic pumpkin in the kitchen. The lemonade is in the refrigerator. I left everything ready for us. I knew you'd need some refreshments after your long flight." She smiled. "We can have them on the table out back—with Jennifer."

Nancy hurried over to give the woman a hug. "Thank you, Mrs. . . . Grace," she whispered.

Ned returned from checking on Jennifer and Brewster and asked, "Shall I take the suitcases to our rooms? If you'll tell me where you want us . . ."

Grace looked around. "I almost forgot that," she admitted. "You'll be in the room at the end of that hall, Ned." She pointed. "Nancy and Jennifer can share the front bedroom upstairs. The first door to the right at the top of the stairs."

"Don't be too long," Nancy teased, "or Jennifer and I will eat all the cookies."

Grace joined Nancy just as she finished filling the glasses and was taking cookies from the huge pumpkin cookie jar. She was frowning.

"Dave Hill is going to check into it," she said, "but he didn't sound too hopeful. Everyone is so busy during the rodeo."

"What about Jennifer?" Nancy asked. "They won't take her away, will they?"

Grace smiled. "I told Dave he could count on me to take care of her till her mother is found."

Nancy sighed. "I just hope that is soon," she said.

"Where do you think we should start looking?" Ned asked, joining them in time to take the tray that Nancy had filled.

"I think we should drive by the Buckman house," Nancy suggested. "I noticed the address when I was trying to call her from the airport."

"I thought you said the phone was disconnected," Ned reminded her.

"Maybe she's just returned from somewhere and hasn't had the phone turned on," Nancy countered. "Or her neighbors might be able to tell us something."

"That's a good thought," Grace agreed. "I don't really watch my neighbors, but I usually know when they're called out of town or something."

The romp with Brewster seemed to have made Jennifer feel much better. As soon as she finished a glass of lemonade and several cookies, she was quite content to settle on the floor in front of the television set, one arm around the collie's furry neck. Nancy and Ned left her there under Grace's watchful eye, while they borrowed her small coupe and drove into Cheyenne, seeking the address from the phone book.

When they finally found the street, Nancy felt her hopes ebbing. The house was a small, attractive one, but the lawn was shaggy and brown from lack of care and the windows had the blind look of drawn shades.

"It doesn't seem very promising, does it?" Ned observed.

Nancy shook her head. "I guess we'd better try the house, though," she said. "And maybe peek in the garage windows, see if there's a car parked there."

"You try the door, I'll check the garage," Ned agreed, as they got out of the car, "but if she is living here, she definitely needs some yard work done."

"Maybe she isn't able to do it," Nancy reminded him. "She was in an accident, you know."

Ned nodded, then left her, walking around the side of the house to the garage. Nancy hurried to the front door, noticing as she did that there were several bits of junk mail in the mailbox. The doorbell echoed emptily behind the white-painted door and, after several tries, she gave up and went to see if Ned was having any luck.

"There's a car in there," Ned told her when they met at the corner of the house. "I can't see it very well, but it looks like a fairly new one."

"Then she has been here," Nancy said, brightening.

"Or someone has," Ned corrected. "She could have rented the garage, you know. People sometimes do if they don't have a car of their own."

Nancy sighed and acknowledged that he might be right. "You take the neighboring houses to the east and I'll take the ones to the west," she said. "That way it won't take so long to find out if anyone has seen Mrs. Buckman."

It took longer than Nancy had expected and the results were dismal. Most of the neighbors seemed suspicious of Nancy's questions and reluctant to discuss the owner of the house. It was only when she tried the cottage directly across the street that she got some answers.

"Lorna was here for a few days early in the week," the tired-looking woman told Nancy. "I was real surprised to see her, if you want to know the truth. I thought she might sell the place after the accident, but I suppose with a child to raise and everything . . ."

"You haven't seen her today?" Nancy asked.

The woman shook her head. "Not for two or three days. I expect she left town to get away from the rodeo crowds. A lot of people do, you know. Folks come here from all over just to see the rodeo and the local people leave just to avoid it." She laughed without humor. "Guess that's human nature."

"Do you have any idea where she might go?" Nancy pressed. "It's really very urgent that I get in touch with her."

"What do you want with her?" The eyes were suddenly hostile.

"It has to do with her little girl," Nancy explained. "Do you know anyone Mrs. Buckman might have gone to visit or who might know where she is?"

The woman considered for several minutes,

then shook her head. "I only know Lorna to say hello and good-bye to, that's all, and I didn't even do that much this time. Just waved out the window at her. She could be just about anywhere and nobody in this neighborhood would know it."

"Well, if she should happen to come back, could you give her a message for me?" Nancy asked, sure even as she spoke that her mission was hopeless. "Could you give her my name and phone number and ask her to call me right away?"

The woman didn't look particularly eager, but after a few moments' thought, she nodded reluctantly. "If I happen to see her," she said, "I guess I could do that much."

Nancy wrote her name and Grace's phone number on a piece of paper from her purse, then thanked the woman and returned to the car. An equally discouraged-looking Ned was waiting for her. "Any luck?" he asked.

Nancy shook her head. "She was there the first of the week, but no one seems to know where she went or why."

Ned nodded. "No one I talked to even knew she was here. It's not a friendly neighborhood."

Nancy started to get into the car, then stopped as a blue automobile came along the street. "It might not be friendly," she observed, "but it certainly is curious."

"What do you mean?" Ned asked.

"Unless I'm very mistaken, that's not the first time I've seen that car," Nancy told him, squinting against the sun, though it did no good. She couldn't see the person or people inside, not with the shiny sun shades pulled down over the windows and the sun glinting on the front windshield. She also missed getting the license plate number as the car quickly rounded the corner.

"Maybe they know where Lorna Buckman is," Ned said in a serious tone, as Nancy hurriedly started the car. But before they reached the end of the road, the blue automobile had vanished into the heavy flow of traffic on a nearby street.

Nancy sighed. "What am I going to tell Jennifer?" she asked, well aware that Ned couldn't answer that question any more than she could. There were times when being a detective was very discouraging.

4

Close Call

Though the bright lights of the town and the colorful music and neon glow of the carnival near the rodeo grounds offered excitement, Nancy was too discouraged and worried to be interested. She was glad when Ned drove her back to the Reed house, even though she wasn't looking forward to telling Jennifer that she hadn't been able to find her mother.

Fortunately, Jennifer was too tired by the day's events to notice the lack of conviction behind Nancy's assurances that she would do better tomorrow. Once dinner was over, Jennifer soon went up to bed, leaving the three worried adults alone to discuss what to do next.

"I made some calls while you were gone," Grace began. "Checked the hospitals, things like that. There's no record of Lorna Buckman being treated anywhere in Cheyenne."

"I just don't know where to look next," Nancy admitted. "I'm beginning to feel haunted. First, Clarinda Winthrop disappeared forty years ago and now Lorna Buckman seems to have done the same thing."

Grace shook her head. "I just don't see how a mother could leave a child like Jennifer on her own this way. She wouldn't have any way of knowing that you were flying with the girl. Suppose she'd come into Cheyenne all alone?"

Nancy shuddered, then got up to move restlessly about the room.

"Would you like to go for a walk?" Ned suggested.

Nancy nodded. "I really think I need one," she admitted. "I'm much too restless to sleep right now."

"Grace?" Ned asked.

Grace Reed shook her head. "Why don't you take Brewster?" she suggested. "He'd love a walk, I'm sure."

The night was cool and a breeze ruffled Nancy's titian hair. The stars seemed extra close and bright once they looked away from the glow of Cheyenne's many lights. "I think we should take Jennifer to the parade tomorrow," Ned said as they followed the white plume of the collie's tail along a rough path.

"Oh, Ned, what about searching for her mother?" Nancy asked.

"You said you didn't know where to start," he reminded her. "Maybe a little relaxation will do you both some good. Besides, I think she'd enjoy it and I know I would."

Nancy responded to his teasing grin. "So would I," she admitted. "And that's a good idea. We can always start our search after the parade."

The July sun was hot the next morning as they waited on the crowded curb. Nancy looked longingly at the shade near the storefronts behind them, but knew she couldn't relinquish her position if she wanted to see the parade. Jennifer, somewhat recovered, was already dancing off the curb into the street to look for the first riders.

"Should be coming pretty soon," Ned announced, checking his watch. "It's past ten."

"Parades are always late," Jennifer informed him.

"Not too late," Nancy said as her sharp ears caught the distant sounds of a band. "It must be coming now."

A shout from the crowd confirmed her statement and everyone pressed forward as the first riders came into view, their horses dancing wildly as the wind caught the flags their riders carried and made them snap around the horses' ears.

One of the horses, a big bay, reared and slipped on the unfamiliar pavement. Nancy pulled Jennifer back quickly as the rider spurred the horse forward, then steadied him so he didn't fall.

Wagons, buckboards, carriages, and even stagecoaches followed each other along the parade route. Teams, nervous and wet with sweat from the excitement and unfamiliar crowds, danced and jumped from the sounds of firecrackers and the blanks fired by a number of riders costumed as possemen or desperados.

There were floats depicting Old West scenes. One featured square dancers who swirled and danced on the wide bed of a truck as the music and voice of the dance caller filled the air.

"That looks like fun," Ned commented as an old-fashioned chuckwagon barbecue scene passed, filling the air with an all-too-authentic scent of cooking meat. "I wonder how you get to be on a float."

"I'd like to ride in a wagon," Nancy said, her attention caught by a buggy that was passing. "Look at those dresses. They must be genuine antiques, too."

"I'd rather ride a horse," Jennifer stated, then began waving furiously to several youngsters who were passing. They waved back, calling her name.

Nancy smiled, happy to see that Jennifer had momentarily forgotten her mother's disappearance, then realized that she might be overlooking a clue. "Who were those children, Jennifer?" she asked.

"Becky and Andy from the Pony Club," was the quick answer, though Jennifer didn't even look her way.

"Would their parents know your mother?" Nancy asked.

This time Jennifer turned from the parade, her eyes bright with excitement. "Sure they would," she replied. "We used to go on picnics and rides together and our mothers always had meetings about the food and everything."

"After the parade, I want you to give me as many names of the Club members as you can remember," Nancy told the little girl. "One of them may know where your mother is."

A mounted sheriff's posse came abreast of them, shouting and firing blanks into the bright, hot air. Shouts from the crowd made it plain that the men were well-known and liked. One rider stopped to take a young boy in front of him on his horse.

The next wagon had a sharpshooter on board and he spent his time tossing light-colored balls into the air, shooting them over the crowd so that when they shattered, the brightly wrapped candies inside fell to the eagerly waiting children.

Nancy laughed as Jennifer disappeared into the crowd with the rest of the children. The young detective started to turn to Ned, to tell him how happy she was he'd suggested coming to the parade. However, before she could speak, a fast-moving body came hurtling into her from behind, striking her so hard she stum-

bled forward right into the path of a prancing pinto.

"Nancy!" Ned's strong hand caught her arm and jerked her back from the flashing, steel-shod hooves.

She stumbled back onto the curb.

"Are you all right?" he asked, his arm protectively about her shoulders.

Nancy caught her breath, then looked around. "Who in the world did that?" she gasped. "And where did he go?"

Ned shook his head. "I don't know where he went, but it was a young man, in his early twenties, I'd say. He had dark hair and a fancy mustache. Why in the world he . . ."

Nancy heard no more, for her ears had caught another sound, one made faint and hard to hear by the blaring of the gaily costumed band that was now passing. What she heard was a child's voice screaming her name!

"Jennifer?" she gasped, looking around wildly. "Ned, where is Jennifer?"

Their eyes met for just a moment, then they both plunged into the crowd, pushing and shoving rather rudely in their frantic hurry, fear for the child overriding their normally good manners. Several people pushed back and made unkind remarks, but most seemed to understand from Nancy's and Ned's worried expressions that something was wrong and moved out of their way.

"Jennifer!" Nancy shouted, hoping that she could be heard above the hubbub. "Jennifer, where are you?" She had a horrible feeling that the little girl might be about to vanish as strangely as her mother had.

5

Rescue

"Nancy!" The shriek came from just ahead and around a corner.

Nancy ran toward it, grateful that the crowd was thinning as she left the parade route. The sight that met her eyes as she rounded the corner shocked her to a standstill.

A familiar blue car was pulled up to the curb, the door hanging open and the motor running. A blond man was moving toward the car carrying a screaming Jennifer, tightly gripped in his darkly tanned arms.

"Stop!" Nancy shouted, racing forward. "You let her go!"

The young man slowed his stride long

enough to look back and as he did so, Jennifer began to kick violently. One of her boot-clad feet quickly caught him on the kneecap.

The man gave a yelp of pain and dropped Jennifer, then hobbled away, leaping into the blue car, which pulled out even before he'd managed to close the door. Brakes squealed as a dozen horns blared at the car before it disappeared into a nearby alley.

This time, however, Nancy made a mental note of the license plate number, then dropped to her knees beside the sobbing child. "Are you all right, Jennifer?" she asked, taking the girl in her arms. "Did he hurt you?"

Ned came striding up before Jennifer could answer. "What happened?" he demanded, his usually pleasant face dark with anger.

"They were trying to kidnap Jennifer," Nancy answered. "It was that same blue car we saw when we went to the Buckman house."

"Was it the man with the mustache?" Ned asked.

Nancy shook her head. "This one was blond and younger, I think." She closed her eyes for a moment, realizing what she'd said, then gasped. "Ned, I've seen both the men before. I just remembered it. They were at the airport yesterday. I saw them watching us, but I really didn't give it a thought."

"Do you suppose they could have been there looking for Jennifer?" Ned asked.

"He said he was going to take me to my mother," Jennifer said, breaking into the conversation as her sobs changed to hiccups. "I thought maybe he was from the Pony Club or something, so I went with him. Then I told him we should tell you that we were going and that's when he picked me up and started running." Tears filled her brown eyes again. "I was so scared, Nancy."

"Did you see an older man with a mustache?" Ned asked.

Jennifer shook her head.

"He was probably in the car," Nancy supplied, her mind working rapidly. "They must have been watching us, just waiting for a chance."

Ned nodded his agreement to the theory.

"When Jennifer went into the crowd, it was easy for them to distract us by pushing me into the street," Nancy continued. "They probably expected to be far away before we missed Jennifer."

"So what do we do now?" Ned asked her with a concerned look.

Nancy looked at Jennifer. "Do you want to go back to the parade?" she asked.

"I don't think so," Jennifer replied. "Not today."

"There are plenty more parades we can watch," Ned agreed. "Grace says there are three to come—Tuesday, Thursday, and next Saturday."

"Maybe we can even ride in one," Nancy suggested, hoping to distract Jennifer now that she was sure she hadn't been injured when the man dropped her.

"I think we all need a nice cool drink before we go back to the car," Ned said.

Nancy agreed. Now that the excitement was over, she felt a little shaky as she realized how badly she could have been injured if Ned hadn't caught her arm as she stumbled into the path of the parade horses. She was very glad to have Ned's arm around her waist and Jennifer's hand in hers as they walked through the crowded streets to a nearby fountain.

By the time they'd finished delicious sodas, Jennifer was calm enough to give Nancy a list of the names of all the people she could remember from the Pony Club. It was a discouragingly short list, since Jennifer knew many of the children by their first names only, having lived in Cheyenne through one summer before going off to boarding school in the fall. The adults she knew only by the names she'd heard her mother call them.

"I'm sorry I can't help more, Nancy," she said. "Maybe I should have gone with that man. Maybe he really could have taken me to my mother."

Nancy shook her head emphatically. "Your mother would never have approved of someone just taking you that way, Jennifer. I don't know what's going on here, but I'm going to do my best to find out."

"Ready to go back to Grace's?" Ned asked.

Nancy nodded. "Maybe she'll recognize some of these names," she suggested hopefully. "Or she might know someone who can give me

51

information about the Pony Club members."

"I just want to find Mom," Jennifer murmured sadly. "I miss her, Nancy. She's been sick for so long and she was just beginning to write about what we'd do when she felt better and I could come home."

"It has been a long time for you, hasn't it?" Nancy asked.

"We were on our way to California on vacation before school last fall. That's when the accident happened. I guess I was lucky my grandmother could get them to take me at the boarding school, but I didn't like being so far away from Mom."

"I'll do my best to get you two back together," Nancy promised as they got into the car.

An afternoon on the telephone proved more frustrating than rewarding for Nancy in spite of her hopes. An attempt to trace the driver of the blue car proved futile since the police report indicated it belonged to someone out-of-state from whom it had been stolen a week earlier. Then, with Grace's help, she did manage to contact several adult sponsors of the Pony Club, but they gave little information. All were concerned and several made offers of assistance, saying that Jennifer would be welcome to stay with them till Nancy located Lorna Buckman.

"I really feel guilty about refusing their offers," Nancy told Grace after she finished the last call. "I know I shouldn't ask you to keep Jennifer, too, not when you've been so kind to Ned and me, but I'm afraid to have her go somewhere else. After what nearly happened this morning, she could be in danger."

"Don't even think about letting her go anywhere else," Grace said staunchly. "She's a dear little girl and perfectly welcome here. She is really a great deal easier to keep entertained than my two grandsons who were here last month."

Nancy looked around at the big, comfortable room. "At least you're not lonely living here by yourself," she observed.

"Not with my children and grandchildren coming by and all my friends dropping in for visits." Grace gave Nancy's shoulders a hug. "Now what about your safety?" she asked. "Do you think you should call your father and tell him what happened at the parade?"

"I wish I could," Nancy replied, "but I have no idea where to reach him. He is supposed to call me tonight, though, so perhaps he'll have some information about our other mystery."

Grace shook her head. "With poor Jennifer's problem, you haven't had much time to devote to Clarinda Winthrop, have you?"

"I really haven't even looked at the list of names you gave me," Nancy admitted.

"I've been thinking about that list and I do believe that you might be wise to contact Mr. Webber first," Grace advised. She smiled. "In fact, I made an appointment for us, if you don't mind."

"Mind? I'm delighted," Nancy assured her. "Where and when?"

"Monday morning at the downtown Chuck-wagon Breakfast. Joshua Webber always does some of the cooking, so he said he'd take the early shift and be free by eight o'clock so he can eat with us. I hope you like ham, flapjacks with syrup, and milk or coffee."

"Sounds delicious and it should be fun, too," Nancy agreed happily.

"Well, I knew you would like to talk to him as soon as possible, but he's very busy with all the rodeo details this entire week. And you've been busy."

Nancy nodded.

"Actually, I was just lucky to get to talk to him at all. He said he didn't remember any Clarinda Winthrop working in the store, but he thought he might recognize a photograph."

"I'll be sure to take them," Nancy said.

The evening seemed endless to Nancy, though she tried hard to join in the conversation with Grace, Ned, and Jennifer. Her ears were always listening for the ringing of the telephone and the call she was expecting from her father.

One subject did claim her interest for a short period. They were sitting on the comfortable lawn furniture on the rear patio after dinner when Ned asked, "Grace, is there any chance of our getting to ride in one of the parades? I mean on a float or in one of the vehicles."

Grace laughed. "Some of the vehicles are promised from one year to the next. In fact, those that belong to families have carried two or three generations in the parades."

Nancy sighed. "I was afraid of that," she admitted. "I was just longing for the opportunity to try on one of those lovely old-fashioned dresses. Besides, riding in a buggy or trap looks like it would be fun."

Grace gasped, setting down a glass of iced tea. "Oh, my goodness, I'd almost forgotten. Nancy, I was supposed to ask you about that very thing." Grace looked guilty.

"Maybe you could ride with the Pony Club," Jennifer suggested before Nancy could ask Grace what she meant. "I talked to Mrs. Carleton and she said that I could ride with them Tuesday." She paused, then added, "If that's all right with you, of course."

Nancy considered the risks for a moment, then nodded. "After what almost happened today, you will probably be safer in the parade than you were watching it." She turned to Grace. "Now what was it you forgot to ask me?" she queried.

"If you'd be interested in riding in the Ferguson stagecoach on Tuesday. Elsa Ferguson's daughter usually rides in the stagecoach with her mother and her aunt, but she broke her ankle this afternoon and doesn't think she'll be up to it so soon."

"Oh, gosh, I . . ." Nancy took a deep breath. "I feel sorry for her, but that sounds wonderful."

"Well, Elsa asked me, but I could never wear

her daughter's dress and I don't want to bother trying to find something of my own. I'm sure you could wear the gown without any alterations."

"That would be super," Nancy acknowledged, "if you're sure. I mean, I wouldn't want to . . ."

Grace laughed. "I'm sure." She turned to Ned. "I'm sorry I can't offer you a similar spot," she said, "but you are certainly welcome to ride one of my horses. I'm sure the Pony Club would be happy to have another rider with them."

Ned looked as though he might refuse, then grinned and nodded. "I guess it would be just as well to have one of us in a position to keep an eye on Jennifer," he admitted.

"I'll call everyone in the morning," Grace said. "I don't want to tie up the phone till after Carson calls tonight."

Nancy sighed and looked at her watch, squinting in the near darkness. "I sure wish he would hurry," she said. "I'd really like to know what he found out when he arrived at that lodge."

"Maybe the reason why he hasn't called is

57

because he didn't find anything," Ned speculated, trying to comfort his troubled friend.

"Then he should be calling to tell us when he will be arriving here," Nancy complained. She was too concerned to be soothed.

Another hour passed and the night became so cool that they moved inside. Jennifer went to bed, leaving Ned, Nancy, and Grace to wait.

Jennifer was long asleep and Nancy could see that Grace was growing weary after the long, busy day. Another look at her watch told her that waiting any longer would be futile, so she reluctantly got to her feet.

"I guess he must have been too busy to call tonight," she said without a great deal of confidence. "Maybe he'll call tomorrow."

"I hope he does it in the morning," Grace said. "We have rodeo tickets for tomorrow afternoon."

"Maybe I'll call Hannah in the morning," Nancy murmured. "Perhaps he called her instead of me."

The young sleuth hoped that she was right, but once she'd slipped into the twin bed next to Jennifer's, she lay awake for a long time worrying. It wasn't like her father to forget to call, not like him at all!

6

Strange Conversation

Nancy slipped downstairs quietly the next morning, aware that no one else was awake yet. Since there was a two-hour time difference between Cheyenne and River Heights, she knew that it wasn't too early to call Hannah. She placed the call and waited nervously as the phone rang and rang. She was almost ready to give up when Hannah finally answered.

"Were you outside, Hannah?" Nancy asked, relieved and a little guilty.

"I was just cutting some flowers, Nancy," Hannah answered. "How are you doing? Have you found the missing heiress yet?"

"Found . . . oh, you mean Clarinda Winthrop," Nancy stammered. "No, not exactly."

"Don't tell me you've found another mystery since you left," Hannah said, sounding amused.

"Well, as a matter of fact, one found me, you might say." Nancy quickly told her about Jennifer's plight.

"Oh, my goodness. No wonder you haven't had a chance to work on your father's case," Hannah said sympathetically. "You just have to find that child's mother first."

"Actually, I was calling about Dad," Nancy said. "I was wondering if he had phoned you."

"Me?" Hannah sounded surprised. "No, I haven't heard from him. I understood that he was to call you last night."

Nancy sighed. "I thought that, too," she admitted, "but he didn't call and I decided maybe I was confused and he'd planned to call you instead."

"No, I'm sure he was going to talk to you." Hannah sounded disturbed. "You couldn't have missed his call, could you?"

"We were here all evening," Nancy assured her.

"Well, maybe he just forgot," Hannah said without any confidence.

"Did he leave a number for you where he could be reached in case of emergency?" Nancy asked, suddenly sure that she had to talk to her father.

"No, he just said that he was going to the Chain Creek Lodge," Hannah answered. "His anonymous caller didn't give him any details, you know."

Nancy sighed. "Well, I guess I'll just have to try to call him, then."

"If you talk to him, will you call me back this evening?" Hannah asked. "I'll be worrying about him now."

Nancy promised that she would, then broke the connection. She was very worried about her father and unsure just how to reach him.

It took nearly an hour and the assistance of telephone operators on both sides of the border, but finally she had a number. When she called it, she could hear the phone ringing and ringing. Once again it seemed forever before anyone answered it.

"Hello." The man's unfriendly tone surprised her.

"Is this Chain Creek Lodge?" she asked, sure that she'd been given the wrong number.

61

"This is the lodge," was the reassuring reply.

"May I speak with Carson Drew, please?" Nancy asked.

"One moment."

An eternity seemed to pass before Nancy heard the receiver being picked up and the same voice said, "I'm sorry, Mr. Drew can't come to the phone right now."

"But this is urgent," she protested. "I'm his daughter and I really must talk to him."

"He isn't here at the moment, miss," the man snapped. "Leave your number and I'll have him call you back."

"When?" Nancy asked. "I won't be here after lunch."

"I'll have him call before that," the man promised. "Now what is the number?"

Nancy gave it to him carefully, reluctant to break the connection. She was very much afraid that she wouldn't hear from her father.

In spite of her fears, the call came shortly and Nancy was deeply relieved when she heard her father's voice. "Dad," she cried, "I've been so worried about you. I thought you were going to call me last night."

"I'm sorry about that, Nancy," he said. "I was tied up here and just didn't get to the phone early enough."

"How are things going? Have you found out anything about Clarinda?"

"Not yet."

Nancy waited, expecting questions about her own activities, but there was only silence on the other end. "Well, then, are you ready to come down here?" she asked, trying to imagine why he was saying so little.

"Not yet. There are still a few things I want to look into here."

"But, Dad, I . . ." Nancy began.

"I've got to run, Nancy," he interrupted. "I'll call you in a few days to tell you when I'll be able to get away. You take care of yourself now."

The phone went dead before she could say another word. Nancy stared at the receiver for a moment before replacing it in its cradle.

"Was that your father?" Ned asked from the doorway to the hall.

Nancy nodded. "At least it sounded like him," she said dubiously.

"What?" Ned came over to comfortingly take

63

her hand, seeming to sense her feelings.

"Well, it was my father, but he seemed so strange, Ned. He didn't ask about our investigation or anything. He just said he was too busy to call last night and that he hadn't learned anything yet, but was going to stay a while longer. Then he hung up."

Ned frowned. "That certainly doesn't sound like him," he admitted, "but maybe he couldn't talk. You know, he might be following someone and if he were standing nearby. . ."

"I suppose that could be it," Nancy acknowledged, but deep down, she wasn't at all sure that would explain the strange conversation.

"At least you know for sure where he is now," Ned reminded her. "You can always call him again tonight or tomorrow."

Nancy nodded, then went upstairs to put on her jeans and plaid Western shirt for the rodeo. It was probably just because of all that had happened that she felt so insecure about being separated from her father, she told herself. She just needed to be sure that he wouldn't disappear the way Jennifer's mother had.

7

Rodeo Excitement

Time seemed to drag after they settled into their seats in the grandstand. The pre-rodeo show was only a teaser for the events that followed. Nancy watched, enthralled as the first bull rider burst from behind the white-painted chute gate across the well-plowed brown earth of the arena.

The huge Brahma made only a few jumps away from the chute, then began a spinning, plunging circle that pulled the unfortunate rider over to one side, then dumped him into the dirt, seemingly beneath the bull's hooves.

"Oh, no!" Nancy gasped, certain that the bull would turn his horns on the fallen man, who appeared unable to get up to flee for safety.

The rodeo clown came dancing forward, his red clown wig blowing in the ever-present breeze, his baggy pants wagging tauntingly at the bull. The bull started toward the fallen man, but the clown was faster, dancing forward to slap the huge beast on the nose, then bouncing back as it turned its furious gaze toward him.

"Most bull riders owe their lives to some rodeo clown somewhere," Grace said, watching closely as the clown sidestepped the bull's charge and ducked behind a rubber-tire-wrapped barrel. "His assistant is in the barrel."

"That's not a job I'd care for," Nancy admitted, as the clown rolled the barrel toward the pawing bull. The audience roared in approval as the bull caught the barrel with his horns and rolled it back.

Nancy looked beyond the bull and clowns to see that the rider was on his feet now and limping toward the safety of the fence. The bull and clown played with the barrel for a moment more, then the bull lifted his head and trotted away as the clown in the barrel stood up and waved to the crowd.

"That bull knows he's through for today," Ned observed.

Grace nodded. "Some people think it's cruel, but the rodeo stock is well cared for and they only have to work a few minutes every day, which is more than you can say for the poor cowboys."

They all laughed as the next bull came crashing out of the chute. This rider was more skillful, staying with the viciously bucking creature till the horn signaled the end of his ride. The clown moved forward immediately, ready to help the cowboy should he have difficulty freeing his hand from the braided rope that was his only link to the furious bull. In a moment, the cowboy was bucked free, landing on his feet and running for the fence.

"If I were going to ride in any bucking event, I'd certainly prefer the horses," Ned observed. "At least they don't try to gore you with their horns after they buck you off."

"I enjoy riding horses," Nancy said, "but I think I'll be satisfied just to watch the rodeo from here."

"I'd like to be a barrel racer," Jennifer said,

bouncing on her seat. "We practiced some in the Pony Club, but you have a real fast horse and the pony I rode was much too slow."

The bucking horses proved to be almost as wild as the bulls had been, and several of the cowboys had to be helped from the arena by their friends. Nancy watched admiringly as the pickup men worked in the arena. They maneuvered their horses close to the bucking broncos so that the successful riders could slide from the bucking horse across the haunches of the pickup horse, then safely to the ground.

"Oh, I know this young man," Grace announced as the speaker named the next rider. "He's the son of a friend of mine."

The bronco was a heavy-headed sorrel that exploded out of the chute, then stopped abruptly, nearly sending the rider over his head. His bucks were wicked, twisting motions without any particular rhythm, and each time he hit the ground, he seemed to land harder than the last.

"He's wonderful," Nancy gasped as the young man somehow managed to stay in the saddle and keep his legs moving forward and back as required by the rules. "That's a terrible horse to ride."

"No one likes to draw old Death Chant," Grace agreed. "He's very difficult to ride, but if someone does stay on for the full time, he can expect an extra-high score."

The horn sounded and the young cowboy reached for the waist of the pickup rider with obvious relief, sliding across the haunches of the well-trained horse and landing on the soft ground as wild applause greeted his score. "He should be today's winner," Grace said, her eyes bright with excitement. "I just hope Myrtle was here to see that ride."

Event followed event. Calf roping, steer wrestling, bareback bronco riding; it was all exciting and a little frightening, yet fascinating, too. Nancy was soon hoarse from cheering and shouting encouragement. Once the rodeo ended, she sank back in her seat wearily.

"Like it?" Grace asked.

"It was fantastic," Nancy replied, "but so exhausting. I don't know how people can come every day."

Grace laughed. "If you'd lived in Cheyenne, you would have had years of practice."

"I'd like to come every single day," Jennifer stated firmly. "I love it!"

Nancy laughed. "We'll have to talk about that later," she teased. "Right now I think we should see about getting out of the stand and going back to the house."

They moved slowly into the rather quiet throng that was filling out. For the first time, Nancy noticed that the sun had faded and dark clouds were moving in. There was a distant rumble of thunder, something they hadn't heard while the crowd was shouting.

"We just might get rained on," Grace observed. "It will help break the heat, but it makes a mess out of the night shows."

"Is that when they have the chuckwagon races?" Ned asked, interest plain in his voice.

Grace nodded. "They used to have the races during the afternoon show, but with so many other events and contestants, it was decided that the chuckwagon races deserved a time of their own. We'll have to come some evening. The races are very exciting."

"We'll have to visit the carnival, too," Ned said, looking toward the rising shapes of the various rides that had been set up near the arena area.

"Tomorrow," Nancy promised.

"Home, then?" Grace asked.

Everyone agreed and, as they drove home, the conversation was mostly about the various rodeo events they'd watched through the afternoon. It was only when Grace pulled into the driveway that she fell silent and a frown marred her formerly happy expression.

"Is something wrong, Grace?" Nancy asked at once.

Grace parked the car before answering. "I thought I left the drapes closed in the living room to keep the house cool," she said.

Nancy nodded. "I remember that you did close them."

"Could someone have come by and opened them?" Ned asked. "Someone from your family or one of your friends?"

"I suppose so." Grace didn't sound convinced. "Several of them do have keys."

"Would you like me to go in first?" Ned asked.

"Oh, I'm sure . . ." Grace let it trail off, then nodded. "So many strange things have been happening," she murmured. "I guess maybe I am a little on edge."

"I'd like to go with you, Ned," Nancy said.

"Be careful, both of you," Grace counseled as she handed Ned her keys.

When they reached the house, Ned turned the key in the latch; but when he tried to open the door, nothing happened. He looked at Nancy, then reinserted the key and turned the knob. The door opened at once. "It was unlocked," he whispered.

Nancy nodded and followed him inside, not at all sure what to expect.

The living room, well lit even though the sun was behind the thunderclouds, seemed sleepily undisturbed. Ned and Nancy exchanged glances, but neither spoke, for they didn't want to alert anyone who might still be in the house.

The search was immediately underway, but there seemed to be nothing disturbed. The kitchen smelled sweetly of the chicken casserole Grace had been heating up; the dining room table was set and waiting just as Nancy and Jennifer had left it. Ned's room was undisturbed as, apparently, were the other downstairs rooms they checked.

"Upstairs?" Ned asked in a whisper.

Nancy nodded and they climbed the stairs together.

A quick check of the rooms up there offered no more clues than the downstairs rooms had. Nancy stepped into the room she shared with Jennifer and looked around. Something about it told her that someone had been here in her absence.

Could I be imagining it? she asked herself.

"It looks like everything is all right up here, too," Ned said from behind her. "I'll go check the basement, then we can call Grace and Jennifer in."

Nancy nodded, but didn't follow him as he went down the stairs. She walked around the room again, looking at everything, but touching nothing. Her small briefcase was closed and when she opened it, the papers inside all appeared to be as she'd left them. But there was still something . . .

Thunder rumbled, then crashed violently, making her start nervously. She closed the briefcase with a sigh and started for the stairs. If someone had been here, she decided, he must have been a very neat snooper.

"Nancy, Nancy! Did you find anything?" Grace's voice carried above the rising sounds of the storm.

Nancy hurried down, shaking her head. "No sign of anyone."

"I didn't find anything, either," Ned informed them as he returned from the basement.

"What about Brewster?" Grace asked.

"Brewster?" Nancy looked around, suddenly realizing that the sable and white collie should have met them at the door.

"You didn't see him?" Grace asked.

Nancy and Ned could only shake their heads and follow Grace as she went to the back door and opened it to call the dog. There was no sign of him. Brewster had disappeared!

8

Warning!

"Could someone have let him out the front door by mistake?" Nancy asked.

Grace shook her head. "The only people who have keys wouldn't do that, Nancy. He's very good about not running away, but I don't like him loose even on these back streets. There's just too much traffic."

"Did Ned tell you that the front door was unlocked?" Nancy asked.

Grace nodded worriedly. "I'm sure I locked it when we left."

"I'm really sure of that, too," Nancy agreed. "I remember."

"What do you suppose it means?" Grace asked.

"I really don't..." Nancy began, then stopped as a sharp bark came from the front door. They all turned in that direction while Jennifer ran forward and opened the door. Brewster came bounding in, his long fur wet from the rain that had begun to fall.

"Brewster," Grace called and dropped to her knees to hug the wet dog. "Where in the world have you been? Who let you out?"

"It sure is a shame that he can't tell us," Jennifer said.

"Maybe he can," Nancy observed, joining the other three in petting the big, happy dog.

"What do you mean?" Ned asked.

"This." Nancy pulled the small, tightly rolled piece of paper out of the rubber band that had attached it to the collie's collar. "It seems he's brought us a message."

"What is it?" Grace asked, but Nancy could only gasp as she read the short note. Ned took it from her nervous fingers and began to read:

NANCY DREW,
THIS TIME WE TOOK THE

76

DOG, NEXT TIME THE VICTIM
COULD BE YOU OR ONE OF
YOUR FRIENDS. GET OUT OF
CHEYENNE NOW AND LEAVE
JENNIFER TO US. IF YOU STAY,
SOMEONE IS GOING TO GET
HURT!

"But who?" Grace gasped.

"It isn't signed," Ned answered, "but I think we can guess who was here while we were gone."

"The two men from the airport," Nancy agreed. "Mustache and his blond friend."

"The men who tried to kidnap me," Jennifer said. "Oh, Nancy, what are we going to do?"

Nancy put an arm around the little girl. "We are going to get a towel and dry Brewster, then we're going to have some dinner," she told her.

"But the note," Jennifer protested.

"Don't even think about it," Nancy counseled.

"You won't leave me here alone, will you?" Jennifer asked, her dark eyes very worried as they met Nancy's bright blue ones.

"I'm not going to leave you till I find your mother," Nancy assured her. "No sneaky dognapper is going to scare me away, Jennifer."

Jennifer smiled with relief. "I'm so glad," she whispered, hugging Nancy before she left to get a towel for Brewster.

"Are you sure that's wise, Nancy?" Grace asked as soon as Jennifer was out of earshot. "Perhaps you're putting yourself in serious danger staying here."

"I can't just let them come and take her," Nancy reminded the older woman.

"Well, we could call the police," Grace suggested.

Nancy considered, then nodded. "I suppose we should let them know about the threat," she agreed. "But I don't think they will take it too seriously. After all, Brewster came home safely."

"I'll go call," Grace said, giving Brewster a final pat. "And I'll see to it that they do take the threats seriously. I'd never forgive myself if anything happened to you or Jennifer."

The evening proved frustrating. Sergeant Hill came and took the note away with him, but his advice to stay indoors and be careful was hardly helpful. Nancy's call to Hannah was also disturbing. Among other things, Carson Drew hadn't called home to speak to her either.

Once she'd hung up the phone after the conversation, Ned suggested a walk in the cool, new-washed evening air. As they followed the trotting collie along the street, he held her hand.

After a while, Ned said, "You know, Nancy, maybe you should do as the sergeant suggested."

"What good would that do?" Nancy asked.

"Well, you'd be safe if you'd stay around the house."

"I doubt it," Nancy observed. "After all, they broke into the house to get Brewster today. Besides, we can't find Lorna Buckman or Clarinda Winthrop while we're sitting around Grace's living room."

"That's true enough," Ned agreed reluctantly. "It's just that I don't want you or Jennifer to be hurt."

"Then our best course is to find out why those two men are trying to kidnap Jennifer. What could they possibly want with her?"

"Do you suppose they could have her mother?" Ned asked.

Nancy sighed. "I guess it's possible, but why? What could they want?"

"Ransom?"

Nancy considered, then shook her head. "I doubt it. The things Jennifer has told me sound like she and her mother lived a rather quiet life before her mother was hurt in that accident on their way to California. Her father died a few years ago and she doesn't seem to have any other relatives besides her grandparents. I don't think they have the kind of money that would inspire kidnapping for ransom."

"What about the grandparents?" Ned asked. "Jennifer never mentioned them to me."

"I don't think they've been very close," Nancy answered. "Jennifer doesn't seem to know a great deal about them, except that her grandmother suggested the boarding school she was sent to. She couldn't even give me their address in California."

"Her father's family?"

Nancy could only shrug. "She never has mentioned them."

"So where do we go from here?" Ned asked.

Nancy stopped and looked around at the pretty night as the moon rose. "I suppose we'd better go back," she said with a teasing grin. "We have an early date with a chuckwagon breakfast tomorrow, remember?"

81

Ned laughed. "You know, we've been so involved with Jennifer's problems, I'd almost forgotten your appointment with Mr. Webber. Think you'll be able to concentrate on such an old mystery now that you have a fresh new one to work on?"

Nancy sighed. "After what Hannah told me, I think I'd better. In fact, I'm almost tempted to call Dad again and ask him to come down here and help."

"You don't think that he's learning anything up at that lodge?"

Nancy shrugged, then started walking back toward the big brick house.

"What did Hannah have to say to you that upset you so, Nancy?" Ned asked, catching up with her.

"She said that she'd talked to Mr. Mathews—you know he's the nephew of Mr. Winthrop. Anyway, he called the house to ask her if we'd made any progress."

"So why does that bother you?" Ned asked. "You said that there was some pressure to hurry with the investigation."

"He told Hannah that Mr. Winthrop was feeling much worse. Hannah was pretty concerned. She seems to feel Mr. Mathews was hinting that

Mr. Winthrop might not live too much longer and must draw up his final will soon. If I can't find his daughter, she will be left out of it."

"Gee, that does make it rough," Ned sympathized. "What are you going to do?"

Nancy stopped and looked up at him. "I won't know till tomorrow, after I talk to Mr. Webber. If he can't give me a clue to Clarinda's whereabouts, I guess I'll just have to try the other names on Grace's list."

"Well, I'm sure you will find her if anyone can, so don't worry about tomorrow," Ned reassured her. "And I know that's what your father would tell you if you asked him."

Nancy stood on her tiptoes to give him a kiss. "You're sweet," she told him. "Thank you for the reassurance. I just feel that I haven't accomplished a single thing since we arrived."

"We still have Jennifer safe and sound," Ned reminded her, "and with the mustached man and his blond friend after her, that's a pretty big accomplishment."

"And tomorrow I really start my search for Clarinda Winthrop," Nancy agreed, feeling restored by Ned's faith in her. "Let's just hope Mr. Webber can offer us a real clue."

9

Clues

The morning was as bright and sunny as Saturday had been and, though it was very early to be going out, Nancy couldn't help feeling a glow of hope. Still, as they drove away from Grace's house, she kept checking over her shoulder to make sure that there was no blue car following them.

Once downtown, however, she forgot all about the threat. Music filled the air and when they'd parked the car and made their way through the throng, the scent of flapjacks and ham made her stomach rumble with anticipation.

Hay bales had been set out for use as tables

and chairs, and there were lines of hungry people waiting to be served. They joined the nearest line and were soon chatting with the other early risers who were listening to the country-western music of a small band that stood on a flatbed truck.

Once their plates were heaped with ham and flapjacks laced with syrup, and they each had a cup of milk or coffee, Grace led them away from the crowded bales. "Joshua has reserved a bale for us," she said. "He'll be joining us in a little while."

"No rush," Nancy said. "It may be unprofessional, but at the moment I want to give this food my full attention. I don't know when I've been so hungry."

"That's what you said last night when we sat down to dinner," Jennifer teased.

"It must be the altitude," Nancy answered, giggling.

Their plates were almost empty by the time a tall, thin, elderly man came toward them. Since he wore an apron, Nancy guessed at once that this was Mr. Webber. Grace's introduction confirmed it and Mr. Webber sank down on the bale with a sigh.

"I swear my feet get more tired every year," he said.

"You could retire from the chuckwagon committee," Grace told him unsympathetically.

"And miss all the fun?" Mr. Webber chuckled. "I'll just complain a little and eat my breakfast, then I'll be fine."

Though she was anxious to question the man, Nancy took the hint and said nothing about her investigation till he'd finished his breakfast and was sipping his coffee. His dark eyes turned her way then and he smiled pleasantly.

"Well, Miss Drew, Grace tells me that you have some questions about someone who might once have worked for me or my father in the store. I didn't recognize the name she gave me, but if you could tell me what she looked like, maybe I'd remember. I'm better at faces than names—especially from so long ago."

"I'll do better than that," Nancy told him, taking the photographs out of her sweater pocket. "This is the girl I'm trying to find. Clarinda Winthrop."

There was a long silence as Mr. Webber studied first one, then the other photograph; then he shook his head. Nancy's heart sank.

"You don't recognize her?" she asked when he handed the two photographs back to her.

"That's not Clarinda Winthrop," Mr. Webber stated flatly. "That is Lindy Thorpe. She worked for us for a couple of years. Right up till her fiance came back from the war."

"What?" Nancy just stared at the man, unable to believe her ears.

"She was a right nice girl, Miss Drew, and a hard worker. We were real sorry when she quit her job."

"Do you know where she went after she quit?" Nancy asked, collecting her wits quickly.

"Sure. Her husband had a ranch about twenty-five miles out of town. They were going to live out there and it was too far for her to drive in to work in the winter." Mr. Webber sipped his coffee.

"And is she still living there?" Nancy pressed, excitement bubbling through her as she began to sense that she was perhaps closer to her quarry than she had imagined.

"What was her husband's name?" Grace asked before Mr. Webber could answer.

"Catlin. Leroy Catlin." Mr. Webber's smile

faded. "And no, I'm not sure where she is, but I don't think she's still living in Cheyenne. I haven't seen or heard anything about her in . . . oh, it must be close to thirty years."

"But . . ." Nancy began. However, before she could go on, someone shouted to Mr. Webber from the serving line area and he got reluctantly to his feet.

"Guess they can't get along without me," he observed with a wry smile. "I hope I've helped you, Miss Drew. I'm sorry I can't give you more current information."

Nancy hurried to thank him for his assistance, but once he was gone, she sank down on the hay bale with a sigh. "Thirty years ago," she murmured to herself. "How in the world am I going to find out where she went next?"

Grace patted her hand reassuringly. "I'm afraid I can't tell you where she went, but I can tell you why she left Cheyenne," she said.

"What?"

"Well, I may not have all the details, but when Joshua mentioned the name Leroy Catlin . . . I had no idea that your missing heiress was Mrs. Leroy Catlin, Nancy."

"Did you know the Catlins, Grace?" Nancy

asked, her spirits reviving considerably.

"Well, not personally, but I do remember that there was a terrible scandal about them and it must have been about thirty years ago. It seems that there was a spectacular bank robbery about that time, and during the investigation, sacks of money and checks were found hidden on the Catlin ranch."

"A bank robbery?" Nancy gasped.

"Mr. Catlin always maintained his innocence, but his wife was the only one who was with him the day the robbery took place, so he was considered a suspect anyway. There was a terrible fuss in town and some people were talking about going out to arrest him themselves if the sheriff wouldn't do it." Grace shook her head.

"How horrible," Nancy murmured. "Did they put him in jail?"

"They never got the chance," Grace replied. "The Catlins just packed up a few of their belongings and disappeared one night. As far as I know, no one has ever heard from them again."

"You mean they ran away?" Nancy was shocked at the idea.

"I guess they didn't feel that they had a

choice," Grace said. "Anyway, they left behind just about everything they had—their ranch, their stock . . . It was sad. Especially later, when Leroy was cleared."

"When was that?" Ned asked.

"A couple of years later, I think. One of the men who actually robbed the bank was caught during another holdup and he confessed to hiding the loot on the Catlin ranch to divert suspicion from him and his friends."

"How terrible." Nancy sighed. "And the Catlins never came back?"

"They may not even know that he was cleared," Grace told her. "There was just no way to find them and tell them what had happened."

"Didn't the police try to trace them when they first disappeared?" Nancy asked, horribly worried that her search had just reached another dead end.

"I'm sure they must have," Grace admitted. "I'll call Dave Hill when we get home and see if he can look up the old records, but I'm really afraid there won't be much to find."

Nancy shook her head. "It was such a wonderful lead," she said. "We found out that she changed her name and that she got married. Where could they have gone?"

No one had any answers for her, and Nancy was glad when, a few minutes later, Grace suggested that they should leave. "We have to go by the Fergusons so you can pick up your costume for tomorrow," she told Nancy.

"Tomorrow?" Nancy looked at her blankly.

"Have you forgotten already that you're going to ride in the parade?" Grace teased.

"And we should talk to Mrs. Carleton, too," Jennifer said. "I have to find out about riding with them and so do you, Ned."

"I should also meet the horse I'm going to be riding," Ned commented.

"Why don't you all go riding this afternoon?" Grace suggested. "My horses can use the exercise, and that will give you a chance to decide which one you want to ride, Ned."

Nancy agreed to the plan, but her heart wasn't in it. She was so afraid that she'd failed. The trail of Clarinda Winthrop, or Lindy Catlin, seemed to have come to an abrupt end and she had no idea where to begin again.

In spite of her misgivings, however, the day passed pleasantly. Mrs. Ferguson was charm-

91

ing, and the gown—a lovely blue satin that just matched Nancy's eyes—was a perfect fit. Nancy hated to take it off after she tried it on.

As soon as they reached her house, Grace immediately suggested a trip to her attic, saying, "I'm sure I have a hat that will go with that gown."

Nancy followed her up into the hot, dusty dimness of the attic and watched as her hostess opened and closed a half-dozen trunks that contained everything from old clothes to a selection of wigs Grace said had belonged to her two daughters.

The hat, when she found it, proved to be a perfect match. Nancy hugged her hostess in delight.

"I'm glad you like it," Grace told her. "I'll see if I can brighten it up before tomorrow. I just hope it makes up for your disappointment this morning. I was so hoping that Joshua would have good news for you."

"Well, he did. I mean, he told us a lot about what happened to Clarinda after she got here. That has to help. And the hat is wonderful. Thank you for finding it."

The long, easy ride in the country after lunch

helped her to lift her spirits, too, though she found no answers in the rolling prairie they crossed. Seeing Jennifer laughing and happy was reassuring and the outing did help Nancy make one decision.

Immediately after dinner, she excused herself and went to place a long-distance call to her father, aware that she must consult with him about what she should do next. The phone at Chain Creek Lodge rang only once before the slightly familiar male voice answered it. Nancy asked for her father.

"I'm sorry, Mr. Drew is no longer staying here," the man informed her.

"What?" Nancy nearly dropped the receiver. "But when? Where . . .?"

"Mr. Drew checked out this morning." The words were cold, the tone unfriendly.

"Did he say where he was going?" Nancy asked, her fears growing immediately.

"He checked out and left no forwarding address," was the reply.

"But . . ."

"I'm sorry, I can't help you, miss." The line went dead.

Nancy sat in the chair for several minutes

after she'd replaced the receiver. Her mind swirled with confusing thoughts. It made no sense. Where could her father have gone? And why would he check out without calling her to say that he was on his way to Cheyenne? And, most important, where was he now?

10

Runaway

Though Ned and Grace both offered reassuring reasons for her father's sudden absence, Nancy was unable to fully accept the excuses. Still, there seemed to be little that she could do, since she had no idea where he could have gone.

Tuesday morning dawned rather cloudy and Nancy was a little afraid it might rain, but by the time they had finished an enormous breakfast of eggs, bacon, and French toast, the wind was herding the clouds away. The sun shone brightly as Nancy changed into the elegant blue satin gown.

She surveyed herself in the mirror. The gown

had a pretty sweetheart neckline edged with faded ecru lace. It fit tightly to her slender waist, then flared over her hips to brush the tops of her feet.

"I just wish I had some high button shoes," Nancy told Grace and Jennifer as they watched her transformation.

"Your feet won't show in the stagecoach," Grace assured her. "That's why you need the hat. People can see it better than they can see the gown."

Grace disappeared for a moment, returning with the wide-brimmed hat that was trimmed with a mixture of blue and white plumes. Though age had dimmed its elegance some-what, Grace had cleaned it well and it was the perfect final touch to the costume.

"I almost wish I was going to be in the stagecoach with you," Jennifer said, looking down at her rather commonplace Levis and red and white checked shirt.

"I wish you were, too, honey," Nancy told her, giving the girl a hug, "but you and Ned will be having fun, I'm sure."

"Which reminds me, I'll have to ask Ned which of the horses he wants to ride. We really must get started soon. The traffic is horrendous near where the parade forms."

It took a surprisingly short time for Ned to agree to Grace's suggestion that he ride Buck, a rather unexciting buckskin gelding. "He's not the prettiest," she told him, "but he's been in more parades than most people have and nothing bothers him."

"Since I'm a novice at parade riding, I'll honor his experience," Ned acknowledged. He looked very much the cowboy in properly faded Levis and a well-fitted brown and gold Western shirt.

The area where the parade formed was a beehive of activity and Nancy was a little concerned for Jennifer's safety in such a busy crowd. However, she soon discovered that the Pony Club was to ride immediately behind the Fergusons' stagecoach. She felt better knowing that both she and Ned would be able to keep watch over the girl.

Though it seemed the chaos would never be sorted out, by ten A.M. the harried and hard-working parade officials had managed to get everyone organized and the flag-bearing lead riders were ready to move out as the bands began supplying the bright marching music. The parade was underway!

Nancy was seated by the right-hand window in the small stagecoach with Mrs. Ferguson in the middle and another elderly lady at the window on the other side. "Just wave and smile," Mrs. Ferguson instructed. "You look like a very elegant turn-of-the-century miss going out to a party."

Once the parade was moving, Nancy leaned out the window and waved to the crowd, then peered back to make sure that Ned and Jennifer were riding behind the well-cared-for stagecoach. "This is fun," she told Mrs. Ferguson. "I'm certainly grateful to you for the opportunity to ride in the parade."

"Riding in the parade is fun," Mrs. Ferguson agreed, "but after about an hour of it, you'll be glad you were born in an era with automobiles and airplanes."

Nancy laughed as the coach bounced and she realized how little spring there was in the sturdy vehicle. "I think I see what you mean," she said.

"Can you imagine what it must have been

like crossing the country in one of these?" the third woman asked. "My great-aunt came west this way with two children."

"I think it would be nice to have a dress with a thick bustle," Nancy joked, patting the handsome, but rather hard leather seat.

The two ladies laughed and agreed.

Everything rolled along smoothly for nearly half an hour. Nancy's arm grew a little tired from waving and she began to realize that riding in the parade was almost as much work as marching in it would have been. Suddenly, however, she felt a tingling of premonition and she began to scan the crowd through the bright paint-trimmed window.

At first she saw nothing unusual, then a man leaped from the curb and yanked at the stagecoach door, pulling it open. At the same time, a second man threw something toward the front of the coach under the horses' hooves.

Nancy screamed as the sharp, staccato explosions of firecrackers filled the air. The stagecoach jerked and swayed wildly and there were screams from outside as the terrified horses and people bounded in every direction.

Nancy leaned forward trying to catch the stagecoach door, but the vehicle was bucking too violently.

"Hang on," Mrs. Ferguson shouted, bouncing dangerously since she had nothing to grasp.

Nancy braced her feet against the framework where the opposite seat had been removed and wrapped one arm around her hostess's waist. The other arm she used to grip the window support. Beyond the open door she could see the people scrambling frantically to get out of the way as the coach careened down the street. The team was running away!

Nancy tried to see ahead of the swaying, bouncing stagecoach, then almost wished that she hadn't. They were racing toward the corner, and beyond the place where the parade was to turn was a barricade. On the other side of the fragile wooden barrier was a solid mass of people, all of whom seemed too frozen in terror to move out of the way of the frightened horses.

Suddenly, she heard the pounding of hoofbeats and a big buckskin horse thundered by the open door, Ned leaning forward on his neck. The reins hung loose as Ned guided the well-trained horse with his knees. Leaving his hands free, he used one to hold on to the saddlehorn, and the other to grab the reins of the right-hand lead horse.

For a moment, Nancy's heart stopped as Ned was nearly jerked from the saddle. But moments later, more riders thundered by on the other side and the left-hand lead horse was caught and stopped. The stagecoach shuddered to a halt, no more than a few feet from the crowd.

At first, the silence seemed unbelievable, for it was broken only by the heaving breathing of the team; then slowly the clapping and cheering began. Nancy gathered her own wits and pulled herself upright, then stepped down from the coach, glad to find that her still-weak knees would support her.

"Are you all right?" Ned asked, dismounting from the hard-breathing buckskin.

"Thanks to you," Nancy answered. "You were wonderful."

"Buck was," Ned said modestly. "He didn't even jump when the firecrackers went off." He patted the horse's wet neck. "What happened to the door? I thought sure you would fall out."

"We might have been badly injured if it

hadn't been for Nancy," Mrs. Ferguson stated as she, too, got out of the coach. "She held onto me and kept us both inside."

"It was the blond man," Nancy said. "He came out of the crowd and pulled the door open, then the man with the mustache threw the firecrackers under the team."

"Jennifer!" Ned gasped and they both looked around just in time to see the girl trotting up on her pony. Her face was pale, but she smiled when she saw that they were both safe.

Nancy and Ned hugged the little girl, though none of them could say a word. Several of the parade officials came galloping up to congratulate Ned for his courage.

"Was anyone hurt?" Nancy asked.

"A couple of people got skinned up getting out of the way, but we were lucky. Your friend here saved us from a real disaster." He shook Ned's hand. "You're welcome on our parade committee any time. We could use a dozen more riders like you."

Ned blushed at the praise, then looked around. "Do you think we can go ahead?" he asked, his gaze more on Mrs. Ferguson and the other elderly lady than on Nancy.

For a moment, the two older women seemed to hesitate, then they straightened their shoulders. "If our ancestors could ride across country in these, I guess we should be able to manage the rest of the parade route," Mrs. Ferguson said stoutly. She looked up at the ashen-faced driver, who was still sitting on the driver's box. "What about it, Jeff?" she asked.

The man looked at the horses, all four of whom now stood with heads hanging, their dark hides wet with sweat. "I reckon you could shoot a cannon by them now and they wouldn't jump," he confirmed. "I'm sorry that I couldn't hold them before."

"No one could," Mrs. Ferguson told him. "I just hope someone caught the idiot that threw the firecrackers."

Nancy looked quickly toward the nearest official. He shook his head. "We were too busy trying to keep people from getting hurt. Do you have any idea who it was?"

"I don't know their names, but I can describe both the men involved," Nancy answered.

"Then you'll need to talk to the police after the parade," the official told her. "I'll have someone waiting at the end of the route. Mean-

103

time, I think we'd better get started. Everybody ready?"

Ned assisted the ladies back into the coach, closing the door firmly behind them. His gaze met Nancy's for just a moment and she could sense how terrified he'd been for her.

"Take care of yourself," she whispered, then watched as he mounted Buck and rode back with Jennifer to take their place with the other members of the Pony Club.

The stagecoach creaked and groaned as the team moved forward, and Nancy took a deep breath before she leaned out the window and waved once again. Her smile was in place and she hoped that it looked convincing to those who lined the sidewalk. Inside, however, she was busy trying to understand what had happened. Why had the men tried to injure her?

Could they have thought that Jennifer was in the coach? Or had they meant to kidnap Jennifer during the confusion that followed the runaway?

11

Night Show

The parade ended without further incident and when Nancy stepped down from the stagecoach, Sergeant Dave Hill was waiting for her. "When the call came in that you were involved in the runaway, I thought maybe it had something to do with your other mysteries," he said.

Nancy quickly described what had happened. The sergeant shook his head. "They must be crazy. They could have hurt a lot of people."

"From the sounds of things, it seems they were more interested in harming Nancy than anything else," Ned observed.

"Do you have any idea why, Miss Drew?" Sergeant Hill asked.

Nancy shook her head. "I thought that they were just trying to kidnap Jennifer, but now . . ." Her voice trailed off.

"Remember the warning," Ned said. "Maybe they were trying to let you know that they meant what they said about someone getting hurt if you didn't give her up."

"Well, I'm not going to abandon her to them," Nancy stated firmly. "I'm going to find her mother and until I do, I'm going to take care of Jennifer."

"I'm afraid we haven't been able to give you any help with your search," the sergeant murmured. "We just haven't found a single clue as to where Mrs. Buckman went before you brought Jennifer to Cheyenne. There is one thing, though. We've found no record at all of a call from Mrs. Buckman to the DeCateur Academy."

"You mean she didn't call and ask Mrs. Peterson to send Jennifer home?" Nancy gasped.

"We can't say for sure," the sergeant admitted. "But we did find that she stayed in her house for several days before she disappeared and that the phone wasn't connected. None of the friends or acquaintances we've contacted let her use their phones either, so . . . Unless she chose to call from a pay phone somewhere, it appears that someone else may have made the call."

"Someone who wanted Jennifer in Cheyenne," Nancy mused. "But why?"

The sergeant could only shrug his shoulders.

Though she pondered through much of the afternoon, Nancy came up with no answers. She was happy when Ned informed her that, since Grace was going to be busy with friends in the evening, he'd gotten tickets for the night show.

"We'll watch the chuckwagon races, then go over and check out the carnival rides," he informed her. "Right, Jennifer?"

"Sounds neat," the little girl agreed merrily.

Nancy smiled at her, thinking that she would miss Jennifer terribly when they found her mother. In the past few days, the girl had become very much like the little sister she'd never had.

This time, the weather held through the long, hot afternoon and by evening, Nancy felt fully recovered from her terrifying ride and brush with death. She donned a bright print peasant skirt and a pretty ruffled white blouse, humming to herself in anticipation of the western singer who was to be a part of the night show entertainment.

The rodeo grounds seemed rather different at night. The crowd was smaller since only the largest grandstand was to be used. A lighted stage had been set up for the entertainers, but the arena was already busy with the pre-show activities.

Junior barrel racers galloped wildly in the clover-leaf pattern, battling the clock. Next there was a mounted drill team to hold their attention with their intricate dancing maneuvers. There was even a band concert.

"Ah, this is what I've been waiting for," Ned said when the first four chuckwagons were driven out of the shadowy complex of pens and corrals and out onto the racetrack that surrounded the huge arena.

"I don't think anyone could do much cooking in one of those," Nancy observed as the small, light wagons paraded past the grandstand.

"I think they must have lost a lot of weight in the translation from trail drive to racetrack,"

Ned agreed. "And look at those horses."

"They look just like racehorses," Jennifer commented.

"They are," Nancy confirmed. "Now, how does the race work?"

"According to what I've heard, that black box in the back of the wagon is supposed to represent a stove. When the race starts, the two outriders are to be standing on the ground beside the stove. They have to throw the stove into the back of the wagon and mount their horses. Then everybody races around the track."

"That sounds simple enough," Nancy said.

"Well, I've heard it's pretty rugged," Ned cautioned. "It's a team effort. Not only does the wagon have to be first, but they can get time penalties if their outriders don't finish, if they knock over a barrel coming out of the arena, or if the stove falls out or is left behind. Of course, this is not to mention how tricky it must be to try to guide and control four racing thoroughbreds pulling a wagon."

Nancy shuddered. "Don't remind me about runaway teams," she said.

The announcer explained the race rules, then the four wagons were positioned in the arena, their starting places marked by brightly painted barrels. The outriders were on the ground behind the wagons ready to toss the "stoves" into the basket-style back compartments of the wagons.

The starting pistol sent the momentarily quiet scene into total chaos. Horses reared and leaped forward. The outriders scrambled with the stoves, barely getting them in before the wagons went tearing around the barrel markers and exploded out onto the track.

"Look, one of the outriders lost his horse," Jennifer shouted, pointing to where the hapless young man was racing along the track on foot, half obscured by the rising dust from the four wagons and their speeding teams.

"That must be his partner," Nancy said, spotting a second young man who'd grabbed the reins of the runaway horse and was dragging it back toward his partner.

The crowd around them shouted encouragement, then laughed as the young man vaulted aboard and set off in pursuit of the vanishing teams. It was hard to see what was going on when the wagons reached the far side of the oval track; but once they came around and headed down the home stretch in front of the grandstand, Nancy found herself shouting with the rest of the crowd.

"The guy that lost his horse must really have a fast mount," Ned observed as the dancing teams were stopped, turned, and brought slowly back to await the announcement of the results of the first race. "He was last, but he wasn't far behind several of the other riders."

Nancy laughed. "That's even wilder than my ride today," she commented. "I don't see how the drivers stay on the wagons."

"I'd like to be an outrider," Jennifer said.

"I think I'd rather ride in a drill team," Nancy replied. "Those kids who were square-dancing on horseback really looked like they were having a good time."

"That would be fun," Jennifer agreed, then added, "Mom likes to square dance."

Jennifer's smile faded and Nancy felt again the frustration of her position. Why couldn't she find a single clue to Lorna Buckman's whereabouts? And what about Clarinda Winthrop? Those worries dampened her enjoyment of the rest of the night show, though not so much that Jennifer or Ned noticed.

"Ready to go try some of the carnival rides?" Ned asked when the night show ended.

"I'm not too tired," Nancy answered. "Are you, Jennifer?"

"Of course not," was the quick reply. "I can hardly wait."

The carnival was like another world. The walkways had been sprinkled with oil and the scent still clung to the air as did the dust that no amount of oil seemed able to control. Still, as they progressed, their noses were tantalized by the smell of frying hamburgers and hotdogs, the sweetness of cotton candy and candy apples, the lure of fresh popcorn and roasting peanuts.

Crowds moved up and down the midway, laughing and shouting above the pleading calls of the barkers at the various games of chance and sideshows. Lines formed at each of the rides as people waited impatiently while others rode the clanking, roaring, stomach-clutching machines.

"What are we going to do first?" Jennifer demanded.

"What would you like to do?" Ned asked.

"I want to go on the Ferris wheel."

"Nancy?" Ned asked.

112

"I think I'll pass this time," Nancy said. "You two go ahead."

"Are you sure?"

"One wild ride a day is my limit," Nancy teased.

"Well, if you really don't want to go. . . ." Ned and Jennifer left the young sleuth and got in the Ferris wheel line.

Nancy wandered on along the midway, watching the fascinating people that milled there. She smiled at the children waiting in line at the pony ride. Once they were lifted aboard the patient ponies, she could see their eyes brightening with dreams. She knew they were imagining themselves to be cowboys and cowgirls just like the ones they had seen earlier in the parade and at the rodeo.

When she reached the end of the brightly lit midway, she turned around and started back, aware that Jennifer and Ned would soon be finished with their ride on the Ferris wheel and that they would be looking for her.

As she neared the Ferris wheel, a huge crowd of people came off one of the other rides, blocking the narrow walkway.

"Honestly, they should have made the path

wider," Nancy muttered, stepping off the pathway into the shadows between two of the exhibit tents. She had to wait there for the throng to pass.

At that moment, a movement in the crowd near the Ferris wheel caught her eye and Nancy gasped as she recognized the tall, dark, mustached form of one of her enemies. Her heart skipped a beat as she realized that he was watching the Ferris wheel, which even now was slowing to discharge its riders!

12

Danger

Nancy took only a moment, then made her decision and plunged into the crowd, pushing her way through the people till she was close behind the dark-haired man. There she stopped, hoping that this time she and Ned could capture the man and finally get some answers.

She soon spotted Ned and Jennifer and when Ned looked her way, she quickly signaled his attention toward the waiting man, mouthing the words, "It's him."

Ned's slight nod was answer enough. She waited, holding herself ready, sure that the man would make his move as soon as Jennifer and Ned left the Ferris wheel.

To her surprise, nothing happened as Ned and Jennifer moved away from the ride. Nancy watched as Ned hesitated for a moment, then began moving slowly along the midway, Jennifer's hand firmly in his. The dark man slipped into the crowd behind them and, after a second of hesitation, Nancy followed him.

She'd taken only a few steps when the sound of her name forced her attention away from the man she was pursuing.

"Nancy Drew, over here." The woman's voice was soft and seemed to come from the shadowed area between the concessions where Nancy had stopped before. Nancy deliberated only a moment, then made her way in that direction.

"Over here, behind the stand," the voice directed and Nancy followed it, her curiosity fully aroused. Who in the world could be calling to her?

Suddenly, strong arms grabbed her from behind and a hand was quickly clapped over her mouth to keep her from screaming. Nancy struggled furiously, but a second pair of hands gripped her arms and there was nothing she could do.

"Get out of Cheyenne, snoop," a male voice breathed in her ear. "If you don't leave now, you are going to get hurt."

Nancy tried to bite the hand over her mouth, but before she could do anything, something struck the side of her head and the darkness closed in around her. She was aware of nothing until she heard Ned's voice calling her name, seemingly from a great distance.

Nancy opened her eyes and tried to look around, but there was only darkness. Her head ached and she seemed to be lying on something both cold and hard.

"Nancy! Nancy, where are you?" Ned's call was louder now.

"Ned?" Her voice was a funny croak, not at all the way it should be. She turned her head and saw the glow of the midway just beyond the dark bulk of a building of some sort.

Memory rushed back and she tried to get to her feet. By the time Ned reached her, she was leaning against the corner post of the concession stand, her head spinning and pounding.

"Nancy, what happened?" Ned demanded. "We've been frantic!"

"Jennifer?" Nancy looked around and was relieved to see the little girl standing just behind Ned. "I thought they might have tried to take you again."

"Evidently they were more interested in you," Ned commented. "What are you doing out here, anyway? I thought you were following our friend with the mustache."

Nancy explained quickly, finishing, "I was really foolish to come away from the crowd, but I never dreamed there was a woman involved. She and the blond man must have been waiting together back here."

"Well, I think we'd better get you to the house, then we can call Sergeant Hill." Ned took her arm, pulling her gently against his side so he could support her as they made their way back to where they'd left the car.

Sergeant Hill was, indeed, upset by Nancy's report and once again advised her to be more cautious. After he left, Nancy gladly obeyed Grace's orders and went directly to bed. Two vicious attacks in one day had left her feeling both battered and weary.

Grace came up to Nancy's room early the next morning and, since Jennifer was still sleeping, signaled Nancy to follow her down the hall to one of the spare bedrooms.

"Nancy, I'm really concerned," she began once they were there, a frown marring her pleasant face. "What happened with Brewster might not have seemed like a serious threat, but after what they did during the parade and then last night . . . You can't go on risking your life this way. I only wish I could get in touch with your father. I'm sure he wouldn't approve."

"What else can I do?" Nancy asked. "I can't just abandon Jennifer, can I?"

Grace shook her head. "No, of course not, but the police . . ."

"Haven't the slightest idea where to look for her mother," Nancy finished.

"Do you?"

Nancy sighed. "Not really," she admitted, "but I have a feeling that I must be getting close."

"Why do you think that?"

"The way those men are acting. They must see me as a real threat to them to do what they did last night. I mean, it would have been easier for them to just make another attempt to kidnap Jennifer. In that crowd, though, they might have been afraid they'd lose control of her and she'd make a scene."

"So what do you plan to do?" Grace asked, her tone telling Nancy that she was in reluctant agreement with what the young detective had just said.

"Well, first I think I'll talk to Jennifer about going over to the house she and her mother lived in. I know she doesn't have a key to the place, but it is her home, so I don't see why anyone should object to our going inside and looking around, do you?"

Grace shook her head.

"Then I was wondering, do you know what happened to the things Clarinda and Leroy Catlin left behind? You said that they left suddenly, so I don't imagine they could have taken very much with them."

"True, but considering the years that have gone by since, who's to say that the place wasn't taken over by the state or even vandalized?"

"I'll see if I can find out," Grace said. "Some of my friends might know."

"There just might be a clue hidden in what they left behind," Nancy murmured. "Besides, there really isn't much else I can try, is there?"

Grace smiled at her, her eyes sparkling. "It sounds to me like you've really been thinking about your mysteries and you are going to have a busy time today."

Nancy nodded. "I think it's time we started making things happen instead of just waiting around to see what comes next."

"I'll go and make some calls while you get dressed," Grace promised, getting to her feet. "We can make plans over breakfast."

13

Discoveries

Grace was bubbling with news by the time Nancy came downstairs. "I think we're in luck, Nancy," she said as they all sat down to a breakfast of waffles and sausages. "It seems that most of the Catlins' belongings are still on their ranch."

"How can that be?" Ned asked. "That was thirty years ago."

"Well, Leroy owned the ranch outright and he has a lot of friends in the area. They believed in his innocence at the time of the robbery and they were determined that he shouldn't lose everything. They sold off all the stock and set up some kind of trust. They lease the land for grazing and for crops, and use the income to pay the taxes. They plan that everything will still be there waiting when Leroy returns."

"Wow," Nancy breathed. "They must have really believed in him."

"Enough so that they left everything at the house pretty much the way it was when Leroy and Lindy slipped out of the state." Grace paused, then added, "I talked to Bob Westmorelin and he was very eager to help you in your search. He's agreed to meet us out at the ranch this afternoon. He has the keys to the house."

"Grace, that's wonderful," Nancy congratulated her, feeling much better. "Dad was right when he said that you'd be invaluable to our investigation."

"A terrible injustice was done thirty years ago," Grace replied. "I'd like very much to see it corrected, and this seems to be the only way that can be accomplished."

"I only hope we can find something to give us a direction for our search to continue," Nancy said.

"If there is a clue to be found out there, you'll find it," Ned assured her.

"Well, at least it gives us a place to start," was all Nancy was willing to say.

"What do you have planned for this morning?" Ned asked.

"I was thinking we might pay a visit to the house on Costiller Street," Nancy answered.

"You don't think Jennifer's mother has come back, do you?" Ned asked. "You haven't heard something?"

Nancy shook her head. "It just occurred to me that Jennifer has every right to enter that house whether her mother is there or not. And she could invite her friends to join her, couldn't she?"

Jennifer grinned at Nancy, the light of hope bright in her eyes. "Would you like to come and visit me?" she invited.

"Do you think there might be some clue there?" Ned asked.

Nancy shrugged. "Well, Sergeant Hill told us that Lorna stayed there before she disappeared. For all we know, she might have received a telegram or something that caused her to leave town. It could tell us where she went."

"But if she knew that Jennifer was coming home . . ." Grace protested.

"She may not have known," Nancy reminded her. "Now that we know that there is a woman who is working with those men, we can probably assume that she is the one who called the DeCateur Academy and asked them to send Jennifer home."

"I never thought of that," Grace admitted.

"Well, if that is the case, Lorna Buckman's disappearance might be a perfectly natural trip that she just didn't happen to mention to any of her neighbors."

"You mean maybe Mom really isn't lost?" Jennifer asked, her eyes bright with hope.

"That is what we are going to try to find out just as soon as we finish cleaning up after breakfast," Nancy told her, hoping for Jennifer's sake that she was right in her theory.

The house looked more bedraggled than it had the first time they had come by, but Nancy didn't allow that to discourage her. She had come fully determined to pick the lock on the door, but as they drove up in front, Jennifer said, "Do you suppose that the key is still hidden in the same place?"

"What key?" Nancy and Ned chorused.

Jennifer giggled. "I forgot till right now. Mom and I got locked out once a long time ago and I had to go in through the window. After that, Mom hid a key under one of the stepping stones out in back. Do you want me to go see if it is still there?"

"I sure do," Nancy told her, laughing as the little girl went skipping around the house.

"Think she'll find it?" Ned asked as they waited.

"I hope so," Nancy answered. "I know that what we're doing isn't wrong, but I'd still feel very much like a housebreaker, picking the lock."

"You'd be a pretty one, too," Ned teased.

Nancy started to answer him, but the sound of approaching footsteps interrupted her.

"I found it!" Jennifer shouted, appearing around the corner of the house, the tarnished, muddy key swinging from a chain in her hand.

"Terrific," Nancy said. "Let's go inside."

The air trapped inside the house was stale and heavy, smelling from the heat of the past days. Nancy wrinkled her nose. "Let's open the windows and let some fresh air in," she suggested.

Opened blinds and windows seemed to lighten the mood of the house, but the sunshine that streamed in revealed nothing to help them. The living room was neatly kept, and attractive without being pretentious.

Nancy crossed the room and picked up the folded newspaper that lay on the footstool in front of the most comfortable chair. She opened it, noting that it was dated two days before they had arrived in Cheyenne.

"Would you know if any of your mother's clothes were missing?" Nancy asked Jennifer. "I mean, could you tell if she took a suitcase full of them out of the closet?"

The blonde considered, then shook her head. "I haven't seen Mom since Christmas. I don't know what clothes she has now."

"Well, I'll go look," Nancy said. "Maybe I can tell."

The larger of the two bedrooms, which Jennifer had said was her mother's, was not quite as neat as the living room had been, but there were no signs of hasty departure. Nancy opened the closet reluctantly and peered inside. Two suitcases were stacked on the shelf and most of the hangers seemed to be filled.

128

Only when she crossed to the small desk in the corner did she find a clue. A piece of blue stationery was lying out on the desk top alongside an envelope addressed to Jennifer at the Academy.

Hating the necessity of reading other people's mail, Nancy read the few lines written beneath the date, which was the same as that on the newspaper.

> *Darling Jenny,*
> *I'm feeling so much*
> *stronger every day, I'm*
> *sure it will be possible for*
> *you to come home some-*
> *time next month. You can*
> *go to school here with all*
> *your friends from the*
> *Pony Club and . . .*

The letter stopped there as though the writer had been suddenly called away. Nancy stared at it, frustrated.

"Find anything?" Ned called from the front of the house.

"Proof that Lorna never called the Academy," Nancy answered, carrying the unfinished letter out to show it to Ned and Jennifer.

"Then where is my mother?" Jennifer asked, her eyes dark with worry. "I thought you said she might have gone on a trip or something."

"I was hoping that she had," Nancy confessed. "Now I just don't know, Jennifer." She turned to Ned. "Did you find anything in the kitchen when you searched it?"

"Some sour milk and spoiled fruit and vegetables in the refrigerator, dirty dishes in the sink, nothing else. It looks as though Lorna Buckman just walked out the door for a minute and didn't come back." He paused. "You didn't find anything else?"

"There are two suitcases still stacked up on the closet shelf," Nancy answered.

"So where do we go from here?" Ned asked. "Any ideas?"

Nancy wandered back into the living room and sank down on the small couch. "I'm not sure," she admitted.

"Did you say you wanted to get some of your clothes from here to take back to Grace's, Jennifer?" Ned asked, turning his attention to the unhappy child.

Jennifer nodded. "I'll have to try the clothes on," she warned. "Most of the things I left behind might be too small."

"No hurry," Nancy assured her, realizing what Ned was doing. "We'll just wait out here for you."

Once Jennifer was out of earshot, Ned leaned forward. "You don't think her mother left on her own, do you?" he inquired.

Nancy shook her head. "Without taking any of her clothes? Leaving dishes in the sink? Food to spoil in the refrigerator? A letter half done? And her car is in the garage, remember."

"Mustache and Company?" Ned suggested.

"They seem to be the most likely suspects," Nancy agreed. "And they were hanging around the airport when we arrived. They could have been waiting for Jennifer."

"For a little girl traveling alone," Ned said. "Her being with us must have really ruined their plans."

Nancy nodded.

"So what do we do now?"

"I'm beginning to think the only thing we can do is try to trap them," Nancy murmured, thinking as she spoke. "Maybe we could capture one of them and make him tell us where Lorna is."

"That could be a dangerous plan," Ned warned her.

"If they have Lorna, she is already in danger," Nancy countered. "And besides, I can't see any other way to find her, can you?"

Ned had to shake his head. "I still don't like it," he told her, then changed the subject to their plans for the afternoon when Jennifer came out to join them.

"Ready to go, Jennifer?" Nancy asked, raising an eyebrow as Jennifer laid a single cotton knit top on the chair.

"I guess so," Jennifer answered with a sigh. "Nothing else fits."

"That's too bad," Nancy sympathized, then got to her feet. "Oh, before we go, do you know if your mother has an address book?" she asked. "I forgot to look in the desk."

"She has one all right, but she always kept it in her purse," Jennifer responded.

"I didn't see a purse anywhere," Ned said. "Did you?"

Nancy and Jennifer shook their heads. "Maybe we should check around, just to be sure," Nancy suggested.

"I'll go look in the desk," Jennifer volunteered.

"If you find any old letters, bring them, too," Nancy called after her. "Maybe we can get some addresses, someone else we can contact."

There was no sign of Lorna Buckman's purse in any of the rooms Nancy searched, which she felt was rather reassuring. A woman leaving on her own would be sure to take her purse with her; a woman being kidnapped might not be allowed to take it, she reasoned.

"No address book," Jennifer said as she emerged from the bedroom. "And no purse anywhere in there, but I did find this. It's from my grandmother." She handed Nancy an envelope.

Nancy opened it, then looked at Jennifer. "No letter?" she asked.

Jennifer shook her head. "Mom throws the letters away as soon as she answers them. The envelope was stuck in the corner of the drawer; that's why it wasn't gone, too."

"There isn't even a return address," Nancy said with a sigh as she turned the envelope over and checked the back. "Just a Los Angeles postmark."

"I'm sorry I don't know the address," Jennifer murmured. "It's just that my grandparents had to move last winter and I don't remember the new address."

Nancy went to the little girl at once and put a consoling arm around her shoulders. "We'll find your mother, don't worry," she promised, hoping that the words were true.

"Well, we'd better get going," Ned interrupted. "We're supposed to drop Jennifer off at the Carletons' by eleven, you know."

"Right," Nancy said, tucking the envelope into her pocket. She gave the living room a last, long look, then moved to close the windows and drapes so that everything was the way they'd found it.

As she did so, her resolve hardened. There had to be a way to bring Lorna Buckman home and she had to find it. Time could be running out for Jennifer and for her mother!

14

Clarinda

The Catlin ranch was a thirty-minute drive from Grace's house, thanks to the heavy traffic. Nancy made the trip in nearly complete silence, her mind busy with plans. Nothing she could think of, however, seemed satisfactory, and after she discarded each one, she felt more depressed.

Once they reached the ranch, she saw little to lift her spirits, for it was far more rundown and neglected-looking than the small house in town had been. Grace sighed as she got out of the car and waved a greeting to a portly, balding man who appeared to be in his sixties.

"It doesn't look like they'd have much to

come back to now, does it?" she observed.

"In the last thirty years, I suppose they've built a new life somewhere else, anyway," Nancy said.

Introductions were made and Mr. Westmorelin led the way up on the rotting timber of the front porch of the ranch house. "I'm afraid the place isn't in very good shape, Miss Drew," he acknowledged. "There was a time when we took care of the ranch house and really hoped that Leroy and Lindy would come back, but after so long . . ."

"We understand, Mr. Westmorelin," Nancy assured him.

"Actually, I'm really surprised that anyone was still interested enough in the Catlins to hire you to find them," he said, curiosity bright in his eyes.

Nancy hesitated for a moment, then decided that there really wasn't any point in secrecy. "I'm not exactly looking for the Catlins," she admitted. "I'm seeking Clarinda Winthrop. Her father is old and ill and he wants to see her and perhaps mend the breach between them before he dies."

"But . . ." Mr. Westmorelin frowned. "What

136

does that have to do with Leroy and Lindy and finding them?"

"According to Joshua Webber, Lindy Catlin is really the missing Clarinda Winthrop," Grace supplied.

"You mean Lindy wasn't her real name?" Mr. Westmorelin looked skeptical. "That's pretty strange, Miss Drew."

"I believe she changed her name when she first arrived in Cheyenne," Nancy told him. "She was probably afraid that her father would try to find her and force her to return home."

"Her father. But I thought that she and Leroy were going to her people when they left here after the robbery," Mr. Westmorelin protested.

"What made you think that?" Nancy asked, instantly alert for a clue.

"Well, I promised never to say anything about them slipping away like they did, but now . . . Heck, Miss Drew, I helped them load up that old station wagon. Leroy himself told me that they were going to go to her family for help."

"They couldn't have done that," Nancy said. "According to Mr. Winthrop, he disinherited his daughter because of her involvement with

Mr. Catlin. I'm sure he'd be the last person they would turn to when her husband was in trouble."

"Is this Mr. Winthrop living in California?" Mr. Westmorelin asked.

Nancy shook her head. "He lives on an estate near River Heights. Why do you ask that?"

Mr. Westmorelin looked guilty. "That's something else I never told anybody at the time . . . or since, for that matter. Leroy had a couple of maps on the car seat—California maps."

"And you think that was where they were heading?" Ned asked.

Mr. Westmorelin nodded.

"Do you know anything else?" Nancy queried. "Anything at all?"

The man thought for several minutes, then shook his head. "I wish I could help you, Miss Drew, but if I'd had any idea where they were, I would have started a search myself once Leroy's name was cleared of the suspicion over the bank holdup. He loved this old place, really loved it." He sighed. "Of course, he wouldn't be too crazy about it if he could see the way it looks now; but at that time . . ."

Mr. Westmorelin unlocked the door and

pushed it open, ignoring the creaking protests of the hinges. There was a distant sound of scampering feet that made Nancy reluctant to enter, but she steeled herself and stepped into the dusty, dark interior.

"I'm afraid there isn't any electricity anymore, but there should be some lanterns around and we can open all the shutters." Mr. Westmorelin moved efficiently to admit both light and fresh air, then lit the lanterns.

Nancy thanked him profusely.

The inside of the ranch house had once been comfortable and attractive, but time and the owners of the scampering feet had reduced it to near ruin. The padded furniture had been shredded for nesting, papers were scattered about, and dust and dirt lay like a pall over the scene. Nancy stared at it with a sinking feeling, her hopes of finding any clues dissolving around her.

"Where do you want us to start?" Grace asked. "And what exactly are we looking for?"

Nancy controlled her disappointment firmly, straightening her shoulders. "If you and Mr. Westmorelin could search this room, Ned can take the kitchen and I'll start in the bedrooms," she instructed. "And I really don't know what we are looking for. Anything with a name on it or an address, anything that might give us a direction to start a new search."

"I'm not sure there is anything left to find," Grace observed, as she touched an old magazine with the toe of her sandal and watched it disintegrate.

"We have to try," Nancy told them, picking up a lantern and heading toward the rear of the room. "Are the bedrooms this way?" she asked.

"Right down that hall," Mr. Westmorelin confirmed. "They only used the front two, though. One for them and one for the baby."

"Baby?" Nancy stopped. "You mean that they had a child?"

"Sure did. A little girl," Mr. Westmorelin replied. "Cute little tyke. Lena, Lana, something like that."

Nancy smiled. "So Mr. Winthrop has a grandchild somewhere," she said. "I think he'd like to know that. I'll call Hannah tonight and ask her to let him know. Maybe that will make him feel better since I haven't had any other good news for him."

"Maybe she will have heard from your father,

too," Grace suggested. "I know how anxious you are to know where he is."

"That's for sure," Nancy agreed, her pleasant mood fading a little at the reminder of her father and his mysterious lack of communication.

Nancy moved down the dark hall and opened the first door she came to. The paint in the room beyond it was peeling badly, but she could still make out the dancing elephants, giraffes, and kangaroos that someone had painted on the walls at crib height. The room had obviously been used as a nursery and was nearly empty of anything, so she spent little time searching it.

The next room was more of a challenge. Tattered clothing still hung in the closet and when she opened a drawer, she smothered a scream as a mouse leaped out of a swirl of fabric, abandoning a nest of tiny babies.

"Sorry about that, little ones," she whispered, moving away from the drawer quickly so that the mother mouse could return.

Nancy gingerly inspected the other dresser drawers, finding that most of them contained a few bits of clothing, but little else. Time-rotted bedding still covered the double bed, and shoes in long-forgotten styles lay on the floor of the closet, but there was nothing else of real interest to her.

Nancy peered under the bed, but all she found was a well-nibbled old book and the remains of a sock. Wiping her grimy hands on her slacks, she stood up and stepped back from the bed, which smelled of mildew and age. Her foot caught in the uneven remains of what had probably been a very lovely rag rug and she scrambled wildly, trying to keep her balance.

"Oh!" Nancy muttered as she fell heavily into the corner of the room.

The floor and wall seemed to shift beneath her weight and when she recovered, Nancy glanced downward. The baseboard had pulled away and behind it she could see something that gleamed dully in the flickering light from the lantern.

Well, well, what have we here? Nancy asked herself. She reached gingerly into the dim recess and eased a small metal box out into the room.

The box was thickly topped with dirt, but the seal seemed tight and a tiny padlock secured the lid to the bottom. Nancy tugged at it without success.

Getting up, Nancy carried it over to the dressing table, searching through the clutter that still lay there till she found an old, rusty hairpin. It took her only a few minutes to spring the small padlock.

The lid refused to budge till Nancy had broken two fingernails, then it fell back with a squeal of protest. Inside was a leather-bound book marked clearly DIARY.

"Find anything?" Ned asked from the doorway, startling Nancy so that she very nearly knocked the lantern over.

"I don't know for sure," Nancy answered, "but this just may offer a clue."

15

Corral Trap

Though Nancy was very eager to read the diary, she helped the others finish their search of the old ranch house. Not surprised when nothing further came to light, she was glad when they could leave the sad ruin. Nancy was anxious to examine the diary in the bright sunlight of the late afternoon.

"What are the dates?" Mr. Westmorelin asked, peering over her shoulder as they both stood on the porch.

"The last one is August 15, 1950," Nancy answered.

"That would have been just a day or so before they left," Mr. Westmorelin told her happily.

144

"Maybe that book will give you some of the answers that I couldn't."

"I certainly hope so," Nancy said, "and I sure do thank you for meeting us out here and helping with the search."

"If you can find Leroy and Lindy, that would be the best thanks you could give me," Mr. Westmorelin replied.

"I'm going to try," Nancy promised him.

"Well, then, I've got to run. I'm in charge of the downtown square dancing tonight and tomorrow night, and there are several things that have to be checked out." He shook hands with Grace and Ned, then took Nancy's hand. "If you have a few minutes tonight or tomorrow night, Miss Drew, why don't you come downtown and fill me in on what you find out from the diary?"

"I'll do that," Nancy agreed. "Ned and I might even do some square dancing, if you allow amateurs to take part."

"The street dancing is for everybody," he assured her. "You'll be more than welcome."

The trip back to Cheyenne passed quickly and, since it was already late afternoon, Ned drove by the Carletons to pick up Jennifer before they went to Grace's house.

The little girl came out to the car grinning widely and almost dancing with excitement. "Guess what!" she exclaimed as soon as she was inside.

"You had a terrific time with your friends," Nancy teased.

"Better than that," Jennifer giggled. "I'm going to be in the rodeo tomorrow."

"What?" Nancy, Ned, and Grace all gasped at the same time.

"The Pony Club is going to do a drill before the rodeo starts," Jennifer explained, her grin widening even more. "We practiced all afternoon. One of the girls had to drop out and they were going to have to cancel, but they said I could take her place and . . ." She stopped, out of breath. Then her expression changed. "You'll be there to watch me, won't you?"

Nancy and Ned looked to Grace.

"Oh, dear," Grace said. "I'm afraid it's too late to get good reserved seats, but I'll call as soon as we get home. There are sure to be seats somewhere."

"Couldn't we watch the pre-rodeo show from beside the chutes?" Nancy asked, remembering what she'd seen when they'd been across the arena in the grandstand. "We'd be much closer there and after we see Jennifer, it won't matter where we sit."

"That's a good idea," Grace agreed. "We can wait for Jennifer at the arena gate, too, so she can join us to watch the rodeo. I'll make all the arrangements."

As soon as she reached the house, Nancy retired to the patio area with a glass of lemonade and the diary. Aware of the need for speed, she started with the final entry and began reading the faded and sometimes almost illegible lines. It was both fascinating and disappointing.

"Learning anything?" Ned asked, coming out to join her nearly an hour later.

"A great deal about Clarinda and Leroy and the awful time they went through after the bank robbery, but not much about where they might have gone," Nancy answered. "It is really kind of hard reading since she uses initials instead of names and she abbreviates a lot of words."

"Then it isn't any help at all?" Ned sounded as disappointed as she felt.

"Well, I haven't read it all," Nancy admitted, "and there are some references to P and D in the Los Angeles area. I'm just hoping that I can find out from Mr. Westmorelin who P and D might be."

147

"Then you think that they could be our next lead?"

"They seem to be the only one I've found so far," Nancy answered with a sigh. "I just hope that Dad is doing better on the case—wherever he is."

"Are you still planning to call Hannah tonight?" Ned asked.

Nancy nodded. "I want her to get word to Mr. Winthrop about his granddaughter and I want to ask her if she's heard from Dad." She looked up into Ned's warm brown eyes. "I'm really worried about him, Ned," she admitted. "It just isn't like him to drop out of sight without at least letting *me* know what is going on."

Ned looked at her sympathetically. "Can the rest of the diary wait till after dinner?" he asked. "Grace sent me out to tell you that she's nearly ready to put it on the table. You can call home about your dad once you've eaten."

"Oh, my goodness," Nancy gasped guiltily. "Is it really that late? I meant to help her fix dinner. I just got so busy with the diary . . ."

"Lucky for you that Jennifer and I are pretty handy in the kitchen," Ned teased, offering her a hand to help her up from the low chaise longue. "Otherwise you might not get any dinner at all."

They went inside, laughing easily together.

Once dinner was eaten and the dishes were done, Nancy excused herself and placed her call to Hannah, hope making her fingers shake as she dialed the familiar numbers.

The conversation was not a very long one and when she hung up, it was with a sigh of frustration.

It had been good to talk to Hannah, but Nancy wasn't at all reassured by what the kindly housekeeper had told her. The brief note from Carson Drew that Hannah had read to Nancy had given the young sleuth no more clues than her own short conversation with him had provided. And neither the note nor Hannah had given her any idea where her father had gone when he left the Chain Creek Lodge.

Without wasting another moment, she placed a call to Chief McGinnis and after explaining her desire to contact Canadian authorities, said, "It seems to me that a request from you might have more impact than from me."

"Don't worry, Nancy. I'll see to it that the police up there check out that lodge."

"Thanks, Chief—and you will let me know if you find out something."

"You'll be the first, I assure you."

The itch of worry stayed with her through the night and haunted her the next morning as she helped Jennifer get ready for her appearance in the pre-rodeo show. Still, she did her best to hide her feelings from the excited child and she happily cheered her on from the sidelines once the Pony Club entered the arena.

It was a simple drill, but the sixteen riders were very impressive as they advanced in single-file columns of twos and fours. They executed circles to the right and left and did two well-timed crossovers, ending with a fast serpentine ride to the exit gate.

"Miss Drew?" The child's voice drew Nancy's attention away from the arena where the drill team was just exiting to much clapping and cheering. She turned to see a young boy standing behind her.

"Yes?" she responded.

"You are Nancy Drew, aren't you?" the boy asked.

Nancy nodded, mystified.

"A man said to give this to you." He handed her a small piece of paper, then turned and melted into the crowd that was moving up into the bleacher seats behind her.

Nancy started to call after him, then turned her attention to the paper. Her heart pounded with excitement when she recognized it as one of her father's business cards. Her hands trembled as she saw the scribbled, unsigned message on the other side.

COME TO THE BULL CORRAL AT ONCE. ALONE.

Nancy hesitated, glancing back to where Ned had moved along the fence to a spot near the gate. The pre-rodeo show was over and Jennifer would soon be coming to join them.

She could see that Grace was already climbing up in the bleachers to hold their seats for them and Ned would have to remain where he was to wait for Jennifer. That left Nancy alone to respond to the summons.

The young sleuth plunged into the crowd,

well aware that it was possible she was being lured into some kind of trap. Still, she reasoned, the stock area was a busy place during the rodeo, so she shouldn't be in any real danger. Besides, there was always a chance that the card had been sent by her father. If he was in some kind of trouble and needed her . . .

I have to go, she told herself firmly. I have to find out who sent this.

When she reached them, the pens and corrals seemed a confusing maze and Nancy hesitated before entering the busy area. Then she saw him! The dark-haired man with the mustache was sitting on the fence on the far side of an empty pen.

All else forgotten, Nancy went through the open gate and started across the pen toward him, sure that he was the one who had sent the card to her. This time she was determined that he wasn't going to get away from her!

"Look out!" The shout came from behind her just as she reached the middle of the corral and when Nancy turned her head, her heart stopped. A huge gray-brown shape of a Brahma bull was thundering her way, horns lowered in deadly attack.

16

Kidnapper!

"Run, Nancy Drew, run!" the man with the mustache called in a taunting voice.

For a moment, she almost took his advice, but the bull was too close and the fence too far ahead. She knew she had no hope of outrunning him, for she'd seen how fast the bulls could move in the arena.

Nancy took one step, then remembered the rodeo clowns she'd seen during the bull-riding. It was a gamble, but as the bull shook the earth, she knew it was her only hope.

Taking a deep breath, Nancy ran two steps, then dropped to the ground and rolled toward the side fence as fast as she could. The surpris-

ingly small hooves pounded by, filling her nostrils with dust, and the cruel horns raked the air where she'd been standing a moment earlier. Choking with fear and dirt, Nancy rolled under the fence to safety.

Other hoofbeats shook the earth as she struggled to sit up. When she looked around, she saw two riders, one in pursuit of the big Brahma, the other dismounting on the far side of the fence.

"Are you all right, miss?" the cowboy asked as he offered her a hand and helped her up.

Nancy took a deep breath and cautiously shook herself. Everything seemed to be in working order, she decided. "I think so," she replied, beginning to brush the dust and dirt from her Levis and shirt.

"You shouldn't have been in that pen," the cowboy admonished.

Nancy opened her mouth to tell him about the note she'd received, then looked toward where the man with the mustache had been waiting. As she expected, he'd vanished.

Before she could say anything, the other rider came galloping back and began yelling at the cowboy she'd been talking to.

"How did that bull get loose, Slim?" he demanded. "What was he doing back here?"

"As far as I know, he was driven into the chutes with the others, Les," Slim answered when the older man paused for breath. "I didn't even know he was loose till somebody yelled."

"What about the rest of the bulls?"

The younger cowboy shrugged. "The chute gate was shut and the rest of them are on the far side of it."

"You mean they just missed shutting that bull in?" Les didn't sound as though he believed that.

"He wasn't standing around outside the gate when we took them over," Slim insisted. "He's a little big to be overlooked."

There was a long moment of silence as the two men looked at each other, then Slim turned to Nancy. "That was fast thinking on your part, miss," he said. "If you'd tried to outrun Old 79, he would have got you for sure. I've seen him hook a cowboy off the top of the fence more than once."

Nancy shuddered, then forced a rather weak smile. "I remembered what the rodeo clowns did," she told them.

"You're a very lucky young lady," Slim stated.

"Now, would you like a ride to wherever you were going?" He remounted, then pulled his foot out of the stirrup and offered her a hand.

"I think I'll just go back to the bleachers," Nancy said as she swung up behind him on the horse. "The person I came out here to see seems to have gone."

"You were meeting someone out here?" There was doubt in Slim's voice.

Nancy took the card from her pocket and offered it to him. He read it, then handed it back, stopping his horse behind the bleachers. "Do you think someone turned that bull loose on purpose?" he asked as she slipped off the horse.

Nancy thought of the bouncing runaway stagecoach and nodded.

"Do you know who it was?" he inquired.

"Not his name," she had to answer, and then her anger surfaced. "But I'm sure going to find out." She smiled with genuine resolve. "Thanks for the ride."

"Stay out of trouble," he called after her as Nancy made her way toward the bleachers where she suspected that three worried faces were watching for her.

157

By the time the rodeo ended, Nancy's spirits were totally revived and her determination had hardened into resolve. "Tomorrow we're going to try to trap one of those men," she announced after relating her close call.

"How are we going to do that?" Ned asked.

"By making ourselves very visible all day. I really think they've been following us all the time, so maybe we can set up a trap with Sergeant Hill. What do you think, Grace? Will he help us?"

"I'll call him in the morning and see what he says," Grace offered. "But I really don't like the idea of you or Jennifer being bait in a trap, Nancy."

Nancy sighed. "I'm not thrilled at the idea either, but it's better than what nearly happened to me today."

"What about tonight?" Ned asked. "Do you have any plans?"

"Tonight I'd like to go downtown and ask Mr. Westmorelin about P and D from the diary. Do you feel like some square dancing, Ned?"

Ned grinned at her. "I'm game if you are."

"Can we go along and watch?" Jennifer

158

asked, looking up at Nancy, then turning to Grace.

"I don't see why not," Grace answered. "I love to watch the dancers and downtown Cheyenne is always exciting during Frontier Days."

That evening, the downtown area was thronged with people slowing the traffic to a crawl, but Grace easily directed them to a parking lot where they could leave the car. Nancy looked around as they walked away from the lot, trying hard to spot any car that might have been following them; but the traffic was too heavy and the crowds on the sidewalk blocked much of her view.

"All we have to do is follow the music," Ned told them and Nancy had to agree. The familiar music and easy authority of the square-dance caller's voice came clearly on the night breeze.

The roped-off area of the street was already filled with swirling dancers, and it was quite a while before a couple signaled their desire to leave the group they were dancing with and Nancy and Ned were able to take their place.

159

During the time they were waiting, Nancy had a few minutes with Mr. Westmorelin and she quickly confided what she'd read in the diary.

"P and D, huh?" He frowned. "Boy, that is hard. It's been a lot of years, you know."

"I realize that," Nancy assured him. "I just didn't know anyone else to ask."

"Did she say anything about them, something that would give me a clue?"

"There was something about living on a citrus ranch, I think."

"Pete and Diane," Mr. Westmorelin said, snapping his fingers. "They lived on the Catlin ranch for about a year. There's a little cabin in a canyon about four or five miles beyond the house. I didn't take you there to search because Lindy and Leroy never lived in it."

"Would you have a last name and an address for Pete and Diane?" Nancy asked.

"Not with me, but I'm sure it's on our old Christmas list. It might not be a recent address, but it shouldn't be more than a year or two old." He smiled. "I'm sure they live somewhere in California."

"I'd really appreciate having the address," Nancy said. "If I'm right, they must be the

160

people that Clarinda and Leroy went to for help when they left Cheyenne. They are probably the only people that can tell me where to reach the Catlins now."

"I sure hope you are right," Mr. Westmorelin said. "I'll call you in the morning."

That good news made Nancy's feet extra light and she found herself laughing as she and Ned twirled and danced through the patterns the caller gave them. They were panting into the final whirling steps when a scream brought them to a halt.

"Nancy!" The voice was Grace's, but when Nancy looked around, she couldn't see her hostess standing where she'd left her and Jennifer.

"Something is wrong," she cried to Ned as she ran to the rope barricade and slipped under it, nearly stumbling over Grace's legs as the crowd separated to let her through. "Grace," she gasped.

"I'm all right," the woman assured her. "Two men just knocked me down—I think they were the ones who've been trying to hurt you. Nancy, they took Jennifer! You've got to go after them. I think they were headed toward the parking lot."

"But . . ." Nancy began, hating to leave the

older woman, yet aware that Jennifer was in terrible danger.

"I'll see that Grace gets home safely," Mr. Westmorelin said, coming to kneel beside Grace. "You go after the child."

"Thank you," Nancy called as she and Ned plunged into the crowd, holding hands to keep from being separated.

"Where do you think they are taking her?" Ned asked.

"If they were following us earlier, they probably ended up in the same parking lot," Nancy guessed.

"That does seem logical," Ned agreed.

"But if they take their car out of the parking lot ahead of us, we'll never see which way they go," Nancy commented, her mind spinning.

"There's just the one exit from that lot," Ned said, slowing his pace a little. "Why don't you wait near it while I go and get the car. If you can spot them, we'll know what kind of car they have and which way they're headed."

"Good thinking." Nancy gave his fingers a quick squeeze, then ran to take a position near the exit while Ned raced into the lot, his muscular form disappearing into the shadows of the cars parked there.

Once she was alone, Nancy realized how visible she was and quickly took a position near the side of a big van parked close to the exit. The shadows were deep there, but any car leaving the lot would have to drive directly by the van and would be under the street light for a few seconds—long enough for her to see who was inside.

Two cars drove out as Nancy watched, then a third one pulled up. It was an older car, light in color, and Nancy had to cover her mouth to keep from gasping as she recognized the driver as the blond man.

There was no sign of Jennifer in the front seat, but she could see shadowy forms in the back seat. For a moment, she considered trying to jump in the car, but before she could move, it was gone.

Nancy memorized the license number and watched as the car merged slowly into the traffic. She looked back and was relieved to see the familiar shape of Grace's car. She leaped in, hardly giving Ned a chance to slow down.

"They went that way," she said, pointing. "It's a different car, older and light-colored." She gave him the license number.

"I only hope we can catch them," Ned said, maneuvering into traffic with the ease of an expert. "I just wish we'd had time to call the police, too. I don't want to give them a chance to hurt you or Jennifer."

"I don't think we should try to catch them," Nancy told him, her mind spinning with plans. "I think we should follow them, find out where they are taking Jennifer."

"And if we do find out, what then?"

Nancy shrugged. "I guess we won't know that till we see where they go," she admitted. "I only hope they're taking her to where they are holding her mother."

"You really do think they are the ones who have Lorna Buckman, don't you?"

"It's the only thing that makes sense," Nancy replied, hoping that she was right. "Or as much sense as anything has made since we got to Cheyenne."

"Maybe we'll find some answers this time," Ned told her, then gave her a grin. "After all, this was your plan, wasn't it? For tomorrow, I mean."

Nancy sighed. "I didn't count on them hurting Grace and I really planned on being the one who was bait in the trap. I'd never have risked Jennifer."

"I know that," Ned assured her. "But we'll catch them."

"We have to," Nancy murmured grimly as she peered ahead at the endless stream of cars. "For Jennifer's sake, we just have to!"

17

Cabin Escape

After passing two pale cars that carried the wrong license plates, Nancy was beginning to lose hope. Then she spotted the car they were seeking just as it turned onto the interstate highway and headed out of town. Ned accelerated after it.

"Where do you suppose they could be taking her?" he asked.

Nancy shook her head. "I haven't any idea," she admitted, "but isn't this the way we came yesterday?"

"It sure is," Ned agreed. "Do you think that means anything?"

"We'll find out soon enough."

166

The night closed in around them as the traffic thinned and Ned eased back a little so as not to alert the men in the car ahead. Nancy kept her eyes on the red taillights, but her mind was busy and when the car slowed, she put a hand on Ned's arm. "Go on by," she told him.

"But they're turning off," Ned protested. "We could lose them."

"That's the road to the Catlin Ranch," Nancy reminded him.

"Do you suppose they are going to take her to the ranch house?" Ned asked.

"There's a side road," Nancy said, pointing. "We can pull off there and watch. I've got an idea about where they might be taking Jennifer."

"What do you mean?"

"It was something Mr. Westmorelin said when he was telling me about Pete and Diane." Nancy told him what the man told her about the abandoned cabin.

"Do you really think they could be using that cabin to hold Lorna Buckman a prisoner?" Ned asked when she'd finished.

"Well, we know they haven't been using the ranch house. We certainly would have seen

167

signs if anyone had been in there, wouldn't we?"

Ned nodded. "So what do we do?"

"We can go into the Catlin ranch as far as the house," Nancy said. "The car went on past there—I've been watching the lights."

"Then what?"

"I'm afraid to try to follow them. I mean, they could see our lights and maybe trap us or something." Nancy frowned out at the night. "Why don't we just hide the car in the barn and wait? When we see them drive back out, we can go and see about the cabin."

"You don't think that they will stay at the cabin?"

"I doubt it," Nancy answered him. "They've acted as interested in what I'm doing as they are in Jennifer, so I think they'll be going back into town to see what happened to us."

"Won't they be surprised when they can't find us," Ned murmured with a chuckle as he drove down the narrow road to where the ranch buildings waited in desolate darkness and silence.

It didn't take them long to conceal the car in the old barn. After they closed the creaking door, Nancy looked around.

"How about over there," she suggested,

pointing to a deeply shadowed area that had a good view of the road that led in from the highway. "I just hope that we don't have to wait too long. Jennifer must be scared half to death."

"I just hope there isn't another road out of there," Ned observed after a few minutes.

Nancy sighed. "I hadn't thought of that," she admitted. "I wonder how they found this place. I mean, it's perfect for hiding someone, but how would they know that?"

"I guess we'll just have to ask them when . . ." Ned let it trail off and Nancy lifted her head, her ears catching the sound of an approaching car.

Lights tunneled through the darkness, touching the collapsing corral fence and the far corner of the barn. They held their breath, but there was no danger, for the lights came no closer.

"Well, I guess it's time," Nancy said, getting to her feet as the pale car bounced its way toward the highway. "Now all we have to do is follow their trail to the cabin or wherever they went."

"Let's hope it's a decent road," Ned commented. "Grace's car isn't made for really rough back roads."

The road, though overgrown and rutted, proved fairly easy to follow once they left the immediate area of the ranch house. The land was rugged, but beautiful in the clear, starry night, and under other circumstances, Nancy would have enjoyed the ride. Tonight, however, she was glad when the car lights finally revealed an old log cabin tucked under the protection of a rocky wall.

"What now?" Ned asked, stopping the car at once and cutting the lights. "Do you think they left a guard with them?—providing they are here, of course."

Nancy took a deep breath, then opened her car door and slipped out into the cool night air. "There's only one way to find out," she told him, wishing even as she spoke that she was wearing something less conspicuous than the bright red-and-white-checked gingham square-dance dress.

Approaching the cabin carefully, they could see no sign of light behind the two small windows and Nancy was terrified that she'd been wrong. What if Lorna and Jennifer had both been in the car that passed them? What if they'd just come up here to get their first victim?

170

When they reached the door, a new sound broke the restless night. It was a soft sobbing that nearly broke Nancy's heart.

"Please don't cry, Jenny," a woman's voice whispered. "There's nothing to be afraid of, really. They're gone now."

Nancy looked up at Ned, reading his expression clearly in the starlight. "Jennifer," she called. "Jennifer, are you all right?"

"Nancy!" The joy was unmistakable.

Nancy tried the door, but it didn't open. She rattled it.

"It's locked tight," the woman's voice said. "They locked it before they left and took the keys with them."

"How about the windows?" Ned asked, testing the door with his shoulder. It didn't budge.

"I've tried them, they're nailed shut," was the answer.

"Want to try to pick the lock, Nancy?" Ned asked.

"I guess I could try," Nancy replied, "but it might take quite a while. This lock looks as though it was just installed and it's a good strong one."

"Maybe it would be better to just break one

of the windows," Ned mused. "We don't want to hang around here any longer than we have to. You never know when our friends might decide to come back."

Nancy nodded her agreement.

Ned called to the two inside, warning them to get away from the window and to cover themselves with a blanket so they wouldn't be hit by the breaking glass. When they said they were ready, he picked up a piece of wood and attacked the nearest window, first splintering the glass, then breaking the old wood that divided the window into panes.

"Don't you have any light in there?" he called through the open window.

"They wouldn't leave me any matches," the woman answered. "I think they were afraid someone might see the smoke if I started a fire."

"There's probably a flashlight in the car," Nancy suggested. "Grace is the type who'd carry one, I'm sure."

"I'll get it," Ned said. "I don't want to go in there without some way to see what I'm doing. I spread a lot of broken glass around when I broke that window."

While he ran to the car, Nancy introduced herself and was pleased and relieved to learn that the woman inside was, indeed, Lorna Buckman. Ned returned with the small flashlight, which Nancy held while he helped Jennifer, then her mother, to climb out the high, small window.

Only when they were all safe in the car did Nancy ask, "How did you happen to be in that cabin, Lorna? Who are those men and why did they want to kidnap you and Jennifer?"

Lorna sighed. She was a pretty woman, her features very like her daughter's. However, she was frail-looking and even in the dim light, Nancy could see the dark circles around her eyes and the lines of strain in her face. She appeared to be exhausted.

"Their names are Barry and Fred Mathews and the woman is Elinor. I think she is Barry's wife."

"Mathews?" Nancy murmured, frowning. "But . . ."

"I met the woman first. She came to my house Wednesday afternoon. She was asking me some questions about my family. I thought she was another insurance person. Since the

accident I've talked to dozens of them, so . . ."
She trailed off, shaking her head.

"What happened?" Nancy prompted.

"Well, I guess I told her whatever it was she wanted to know because all of a sudden she went to the door and opened it and the two men came in. They brought me to the cabin."

"Why?" Nancy asked.

"I have no idea," Lorna answered and when her eyes met Nancy's, the girl detective could see that she was telling the truth. "I begged them to tell me. I told them that I didn't have any money, but they just laughed at me. They kept saying that my mother had told them different."

"Whatever did they mean by that?" Nancy asked. "It must have been awful for you."

"It was terrible. They left me in that place for a couple of days, all alone. I thought they were never coming back, and I could hardly breathe. Very little air could come in."

"Did they give you anything to eat, Mom?" Jennifer asked from her position snuggled against her mother's side.

"They left me a supply of groceries whenever they came out. They said they could keep me there forever and no one would know. They really didn't even have to lock me in. Since the car accident, I can't walk more than a few yards without having to lie down. There was no way I could escape." Her voice broke and it was several minutes before she asked, "How in the world did you ever find us?"

Nancy explained quickly about meeting Jennifer in the airport and the things that had happened since. She ended by asking, "How soon do you think they will be checking the cabin again?"

"They said they'd see us in a couple of days," Jennifer supplied, sounding more like herself for the first time since their rescue.

"Did you know where you were, Lorna?" Nancy asked. "I mean, where the cabin was located?"

"Yes, I figured it out. I'd never seen the cabin before they brought me out to it, but I've heard it described often enough by Uncle Pete and Aunt Diane. They spent the first couple of years they were married living in that cabin."

Nancy gulped and her voice was a little shaky as she asked, "Your Uncle Pete and Aunt Diane lived in that cabin?"

18

Surprising Answer

By the time they reached the outskirts of Cheyenne, the whole story was told and Nancy could hardly contain herself, she was so excited. "You must be Clarinda Winthrop's daughter," she murmured over and over. "I just can't believe it. I've had Arlo Winthrop's great-granddaughter with me all this time and I never even suspected it."

"My mother's name is Lindy Greenfield," Lorna protested. "It was Lindy Thorpe before she and Daddy got married."

"They must have changed their name from Catlin to Greenfield after they left Cheyenne," Nancy said. "But when we get to the house, I'll show you some pictures of Clarinda Winthrop. I think you'll see that she is your mother."

"I don't understand any of this," Lorna protested. "Who are the Catlins?"

Nancy carefully explained all she knew of Clarinda's life in Cheyenne, then listened as Lorna described her own childhood growing up in California under the name Greenfield. Her memories were happy enough, yet she seemed relieved to have Nancy fill in some of the gaps in her own family history.

"I always kind of wondered why I didn't have any family besides Mom and Dad," Lorna admitted. "I mean Pete and Diane Spencer are only honorary relatives—old friends of my parents."

"Well, you do have a family," Nancy assured her. "A grandfather who wants very much to find you and your mother."

"Where do you think we should go?" Ned asked Nancy as they entered Cheyenne. He slowed a little as they merged with the still-heavy traffic. "I mean, where will they be safe?"

"Grace's house," Nancy answered without hesitation. "We can drive directly into the ga-

rage there, so no one will see them in the car—
just in case the house is being watched."

"Watched?" Lorna looked over her shoulder.
"Why would you be watched? I mean, they
think they have Jenny and me up at the cabin,
so . . ." She stopped and then asked, "Do you
know something about those men, Nancy?"

Nancy nodded. "Unless I miss my guess,
Barry and Fred Mathews are the sons of Tom
Mathews—the man who works for your grandfather. Which probably makes them your cousins, Lorna."

"My cousins?" The disbelief was heavy in
her voice. "But why . . .?"

"Your grandfather is old and ill. Tom Mathews and his wife have taken care of him for
years and I'm sure that Mr. Mathews always
assumed that he would be Mr. Winthrop's heir.
Now Mr. Winthrop is trying to find his long-lost
daughter Clarinda and if he does . . ." Nancy
didn't finish the sentence.

"But why would they kidnap me and then
Jennifer?" Lorna asked. "I mean, I'm still not
sure that my mother is this Clarinda Winthrop
you're talking about."

"I don't know for sure," Nancy admitted, "but

I suspect we'll find out as soon as you call your mother. Now I think you two had better duck down, just in case."

Nancy turned back to the front, pretending no interest at all in the back seat of the car as they drove up the drive to Grace's garage. "I'll open the door," she told Ned, getting out of the car before he could protest. As she did so, she noticed that an unfamiliar car was parked in front of the house.

Once they were in the garage and she'd closed the door, Nancy started to ask Lorna and Jennifer to wait, but before she could say anything, Grace opened the door that led into the kitchen..

"Nancy, Ned, is that you?" she asked, switching on the garage light. "Jennifer!" she shouted as she saw the little girl getting out of the car.

In a moment, they were all in the big, friendly kitchen, sipping hot chocolate and talking to Mr. Westmorelin, who'd stayed with Grace after he drove her home. He was full of questions about Leroy and Lindy and delighted to tell Lorna anecdotes about her parents and their life in Cheyenne before they fled.

Nancy leaned back with a sigh, relaxing a little for the first time since she'd heard Grace's scream at the street dance. "It's too bad it's so late," she said. "I really think we should call your mother, Lorna."

"It's an hour earlier in California," Ned reminded her. "Is ten-thirty too late to call your mother, Lorna?"

Lorna stared at the pictures Nancy had given her, then shook her head. "I guess not," she answered. "She doesn't go to bed early and I suppose she might be kind of worried about me. I usually write or call once a week and lately . . ." She didn't have to finish the thought.

The call proved to be a long, joyous one, but it also presented some surprises both for Lorna and for Nancy. The events of the past had been much as Nancy had guessed, but Clarinda had one bit of news that had the young detective's usually smooth brow furrowed with worry.

"I tried to reach my father two years ago, Miss Drew," she said. "I saw his name in a newspaper article and I thought that he might have mellowed through the years, so I wrote him a long letter. I told him all about my life and about his granddaughter and great-granddaughter."

"You contacted him?" Nancy gasped. "But he never said a word about it. Did you actually talk to him?"

"I got a letter back, telling me that he wanted no part of me or my family. It was plain that he hadn't forgiven me at all." Clarinda's voice betrayed her pain.

"Mrs. Greenfield, your father had detectives searching for you less than six months ago and he hired my father to find you just last week. Why would he do that if he knew where you were?" Nancy asked. "Are you sure the letter was from him? Was it in his handwriting?"

"It was typewritten," Clarinda replied, her tone changing. "I thought it was strange at the time, but the signature looked like his, so . . ."

Nancy sighed. "I doubt very much that your father ever saw that letter, Mrs. Greenfield. I have a feeling that the same people who have been holding your daughter prisoner here kept that letter from Mr. Winthrop. Tom Mathews handles all of Mr. Winthrop's affairs, so that probably means he opens all his mail."

"What do you think I should do, Miss Drew?" Clarinda asked. "And what about Lorna and Jennifer? Are they still in danger?"

"They'll be safe enough here tonight," Nancy said, her mind whirling with plans, "but I think your father might be in danger—especially once Barry and Fred discover that Lorna and Jennifer are gone from the cabin."

"You don't really think they'd hurt him?"

"Your father is a very wealthy man, Mrs. Greenfield," Nancy reminded her, "and some people can be terribly greedy."

"How can I protect him?"

"Well, I was planning to call the River Heights police to do that, but it might not be a bad idea for you all to fly back East together as well. I think it's important for you to see your father soon. You could meet Lorna and Jennifer in Denver tomorrow, before anyone here knows what is going on. Could you do that?"

"Of course." There was no doubt in Clarinda Winthrop Greenfield's voice now. "Leroy and I will make the calls right away and let you know as soon as we have reservations. But is it safe for Lorna and Jennifer to be seen leaving Cheyenne?"

"That's part of my plan," Nancy continued. "Ned, my friend, will drive them to Denver

182

while I stay here and pretend to keep looking for Jennifer. If we're lucky, I'll be able to keep them so busy following me, they won't even think about checking the cabin. Once you and your father are all safe, the police can start hunting for Barry and Fred."

It was after midnight before the entire plan was completed and everyone could go to bed, but Nancy climbed the stairs feeling better than she had in days. Everything seemed to be working out just perfectly.

"Nancy," Grace called, stopping her halfway up the stairs.

"Is something wrong?" Nancy said, noticing that Grace was frowning.

"I forgot to tell you—there was a phone call earlier, from your housekeeper." Grace sighed. "She called right after I got home and I made a note of it, but when you came here with Jennifer and her mother, well, I completely forgot to tell you."

"What did she say?" Nancy asked. "Has she heard from my father?"

"Well, she didn't go into detail, but that's why she called. She said she'd received another letter from him and she wanted you to know about it. I told her that you'd call as soon as you got in."

Nancy looked at her watch and swallowed a sigh. "It's much too late to call her now," she said. "I guess I'll just wait and telephone her first thing in the morning."

"I'm sure that will be all right," Grace said. "I mean, I did tell her that you were following a lead and might be very late getting home."

"As long as she's heard from Dad, everything must be under control," Nancy agreed. "Thanks for telling me."

"I'm just sorry I forgot until now."

"I'm so glad you weren't hurt when they kidnapped Jennifer. We were worried about you," Nancy told her.

"They just took me by surprise," Grace said. "One minute we were watching you dance, the next I was on the ground and they were running off with Jennifer."

"Well, it worked out for the best, anyway, since they led us to Lorna," Nancy commented.

"And now they're safe and the mystery is solved, so you can sleep peacefully." Grace smiled up at her.

"That sounds like a very good idea," Nancy agreed. "Good night and thanks for everything. You've really helped solve this mystery."

"I'm just glad it is going to have a happy ending," Grace called as Nancy made her way along the hall to the smaller guest room where she'd moved her things so that Lorna could stay with Jennifer.

"Me, too," Nancy agreed, but her step was no longer light for she was sure that Hannah hadn't called about an ordinary letter. She was very much afraid that something had happened to her father!

19

Fake Message?

Because of her worry, Nancy woke very early and went down to use the telephone in the kitchen to call River Heights. Hannah answered on the second ring, making it clear that Nancy hadn't awakened her as the young sleuth feared that she might.

"I'm so glad to hear from you," Hannah said. "I was worried when you didn't return my call last night. You aren't doing anything dangerous, are you, Nancy?"

Nancy thought momentarily of the careening, runaway stagecoach and the wicked horns of the bucking bull, then banished all such memories. That was over now.

186

"Everything is very much under control here," she assured the housekeeper. "I just got back to the house quite late and I didn't want to wake you."

"You might as well have called for all the rest I've gotten since Chief McGinnis phoned here and the letter came," Hannah told her.

"What do you mean?" Nancy asked, her fears growing stronger than ever. "Has something happened to Dad?"

Hannah sighed instead of answering right away. "I just don't know," she finally admitted. "The chief said he tried to reach you but when he couldn't, he phoned me instead. It seems that the Canadian police told him Chain Creek Lodge has been closed for a couple of years."

"What?" Nancy gasped.

"That's not all. Let me read you the letter and see what you think I should do." There were a few sounds of papers being moved, then Hannah began to read:

> *Dear Hannah,*
> *I'm writing to ask you to do a favor for me. My lead here in Canada at*

*Chain Creek has come to
a sad end. Clarinda Win-
throp is dead, leaving
no heirs.*

*I will have to stay a
few more days to finish
up all the details, but I'd
like to ask you to contact
Mr. Winthrop and give
him the news.*

*The country up here is
lovely and . . .*

"What?" Nancy broke in. "What did you say
about Clarinda Winthrop?"

"He said that she was dead," Hannah replied. "That's why I called you, Nancy. I just
didn't feel that I should be the one to talk to Mr.
Winthrop about something like that."

"Oh, Hannah, I don't understand," Nancy
murmured, her mind spinning.

"It's just that Mr. Winthrop isn't at all well,"
Hannah continued, not understanding Nancy's
confusion. "News like that could make him
worse. I was going to call Mr. Mathews, but . . ."
She paused. "Don't you think the news could
wait till you and your father get home?"

188

"It can wait a lot longer than that," Nancy snapped. "Thank heavens you didn't call."

"What do you mean?" Hannah asked.

"Hannah, I talked to Clarinda Winthrop on the telephone last night. Her daughter and granddaughter are here in this house right now. My little friend Jennifer is Arlo Winthrop's great-granddaughter."

"But your father says . . ." Hannah protested, her tone telling that she was as confused as Nancy was.

"What else is in the letter?" Nancy asked. "Did he say anything else about where he was or what he is doing up there?"

"There is about a page of description of the mountains, the flowers, and a lake that is not far from the lodge. It sounds like he copied it from a travel brochure." She paused, then added, "Nancy, he never even mentioned your name. Did he call you and tell you to stop your part of the investigation?"

"I haven't talked to him since that time I told you about," Nancy answered, then asked, "Was it his handwriting?"

"I'm pretty sure it is," Hannah answered. "That was the first thing I thought of when I read the letter. I mean, it didn't sound like any-

189

thing he'd write, so I got out some of his old notes and things and compared them the way you do and it sure looks like his writing."

Nancy gnawed at her lip, fear twisting through her. "How long ago was the letter mailed?" she asked.

"Three, no, four days now."

"And he said he was going to stay a few more days?"

"That's right," the housekeeper confirmed, then asked, "What do you want me to do, Nancy?"

Nancy thought for a second, then made her decision. "Absolutely nothing," she replied firmly. "Pretend you never got that letter."

"You're sure?" Hannah paused, then recalled what Nancy had said earlier in the conversation. "You've solved the case? You've really found Clarinda Winthrop?"

Nancy explained quickly about Lorna's imprisonment and their rescue the night before, ending, "That's why I don't want you to contact Mr. Mathews at all. I want Clarinda's arrival to be a surprise to everyone."

"Her arrival?"

Nancy outlined the plans they'd made, but

her thoughts were still on her father. The fact that the man at the lodge had told her that her father had checked out, while the letter he'd written said he was staying on, made her shudder with fear.

"What are you going to do?" Hannah asked when she finished.

"As soon as Ned leaves to drive Lorna and Jennifer to Denver, I'm going to catch a plane for Canada. I'm going to Chain Creek Lodge and find out what has happened to my father."

"Oh, Nancy, I don't think . . ." Hannah began.

"I'll call you from Canada tonight," Nancy told her, "or tomorrow night at the latest."

Within an hour, Nancy had made her plans over the protests of both Grace and Ned, who didn't like her doing things alone. Still, when she stated the urgency and the need for complete secrecy, they had to agree that, in many ways, it would be safer than if she waited.

"Grace has a whole collection of wigs in the attic," Nancy said, explaining her plan to everyone. "I saw them the other day when we were up there looking for a hat to go with the dress I wore in the parade. There's one that

191

Lorna can wear so she'll look a little bit like me—at least from a distance."

Lorna frowned. "How will that help?" she asked.

"The Mathews brothers won't think it is odd if they see you and Ned going out in the car," Nancy said. "Or rather they won't think anything of it if they believe it's me with Ned. Jennifer can lie down in the back seat till you get out of town."

"You're sure they're watching us?" Ned asked.

Nancy nodded. "They always seem to be where we are," she reminded him. "Anyway, I don't think they'll bother following you beyond the city limits. They'll be sure you'll come back here."

Ned and Grace nodded reluctantly. "What will you do?" Grace asked.

"I'll put on a long, dark wig and go next door and call a taxi to take me to the airport to catch my plane. That way the Mathewses won't suspect anything till it's too late for them to cause any more trouble."

"But what about you?" Ned asked. "I know

your father wouldn't approve of you flying to Calgary all alone."

"Once you hear from Mrs. Greenfield that she is safely with her father, you can catch the next plane to Canada," Nancy told him. "The important thing now is to make sure that no one hurts Mr. Winthrop and the only way we can be sure of protecting him is to keep the Mathewses from knowing that we've discovered their plot. I'll call the River Heights police before I leave, and let them know exactly what's going on. They'll have to keep an eye on Mathews without making him suspect anything."

"Could I go with you to Calgary?" Grace offered.

Nancy hugged her. "I'd love to have your company, but you have to stay here and pretend that you still have two houseguests. Thank you for offering."

The plan went forward with apparent success. Nancy, watching from the attic, saw the pale car pull out of a nearby driveway and move behind Grace's car into traffic.

Once they were out of sight, Nancy took a deep breath and went downstairs. Hoping that she was doing the right thing, she donned the dark wig, put on a dress several sizes too large, and, carrying the small suitcase she'd packed for the trip north, went down to the main floor of the house.

Grace had already called and arranged for a taxi to meet Nancy at the neighbor's house. She had only to cross the rear yard and enter the back garden of the house next door. The lady who admitted her to the house gave her a rather odd look, Nancy thought, but wished her a cheerful, "Have a good day," as she left for the airport. Grace had obviously asked the woman not to ask any questions.

Nancy watched behind the cab all the way to the airport and lived in constant fear of discovery until the moment she boarded her plane. Only when the plane lifted off the runway did she feel she had escaped detection and was on her way.

But to what? What would she find when she finally reached the lodge? Was her father still there? And what could she do if he wasn't?

The questions tormented her on the long, smooth flight north, but she'd found no answers. As the plane landed in Calgary, she

194

could only hope that she was doing the right thing.

She went directly from the plane to a car rental agency, secured a car for herself and gained her first bit of information. Her father had rented a car from the same agency when he landed—and he hadn't returned it yet.

The man behind the desk at the agency wrote out the license plate number of Mr. Drew's car and also offered her a map of the area, tracing the route to Chain Creek Lodge for her. "I don't know why you want to go out there," he said, handing the map to her. "The place isn't open."

"I know," Nancy said, without adding any explanation. "Thank you for all your help." She picked up her suitcase, the map, and keys. Once in the small car, she put the map on the seat beside her and set off through the warm afternoon, determined to find out what had happened to her father before the sun set.

The country was as beautiful as her father had said in his letters, but Nancy was in no mood to enjoy it as she followed the ever-narrowing roads into the rugged country. It was very late in the afternoon when she finally found the sign that announced that Chain

Creek Lodge was just three miles ahead down the rutted road.

"Well, this is it," Nancy said aloud to herself as she bounced along the road, not slowing her pace till she caught a glimpse of red-painted roof through the trees.

Pulling off the road immediately, Nancy parked the car deep in the shadows of a grove of pines. Still in the car, she changed into a dark shirt and jeans; then she set off on foot toward the lodge, keeping carefully to the trees and brush so that no one inside would see her approach.

It took quite a while to circle the entire building, but Nancy was rewarded by seeing two cars parked in the rear. One was an all-terrain vehicle, the second a car that appeared to be the twin of the one she'd rented—and bore the license number of the car her father had rented.

Nancy retreated to the shadows of several small firs. "So he *is* here," she whispered to herself. "But where?"

As if in answer, a door opened at the rear of the lodge and a man came out. "Ready for dinner, Mr. Drew?" he asked, the sound carrying clearly in the still mountain air.

Nancy started nervously and peered across the open area, seeing for the first time that there was, indeed, someone lying in one of the lounge chairs that sat on the stone terrace. To her horror, her father's voice came dreamily from the chair. "I guess so. What do we have?"

"I fixed the fish I caught this morning," the man went on. "You want to eat out here?"

"All right." The answer was without interest—almost a singsong—and her father didn't move.

"I'll go get your tray, then you have to take your sleeping pill and come inside."

"No more pills," her father whined. "I'm so sleepy now. No more pills, please."

Nancy covered her mouth to keep from crying out. Her father was drugged and helpless! Somehow she had to free him!

20

Happy Reunion

Nancy moved around the building carefully, peeking in the windows, wondering if anyone else was inside. It seemed unlikely, since most of the furniture was covered with dust cloths and the only light shone from the kitchen.

Pondering her next move, Nancy made her way back to the parking area and studied the two vehicles parked there. Not sure what she was going to do, but aware that they had to escape and as soon as possible, Nancy went to first one car, then the other, letting the air out of both rear tires on each vehicle.

That should slow him up and keep him from coming after me, she told herself.

From her right, she heard the man summoning her father to the small redwood table that sat in the middle of the terrace. She waited just out of sight till her father muttered something about being thirsty and the man went inside to get him some iced tea. Crossing her fingers, she ran forward, pausing at the edge of the terrace in full view of her father.

He looked up slowly and for a moment, she was afraid that he didn't recognize her. Then a smile came over his handsome features and he opened his mouth. Nancy quickly signaled him to be silent. He looked sad and confused as she jumped back behind the log wall of the lodge just as the man stepped out of the door again.

"Here you go, Mr. Drew," the man said, putting the tea on the table.

"How . . . how long do I have to stay here?" her father asked.

"A couple more days should do it," the man answered. "Don't worry now. You've cooperated and when the time comes, you'll be turned loose."

"Why are you doing this?"

"Don't ask so many questions," the man

snapped. "You just keep being good and nobody is going to get hurt."

Nancy caught her lower lip between her
teeth, reassured that her father's mind was still
clear enough that he hadn't mentioned her to
his jailer, but terrified at what the continued
drugging might do to him. But how could she
get him away? She looked around.

Her eyes were drawn to the small shed that
stood a short distance from the lodge. Nancy
felt in her pocket for the book of matches that
she'd brought with her. She scuffed a toe in the
rough grass and saw that it was already damp
with evening dew. The land around the shed
was fairly clear, too. No trees and few tufts of
grass were close and the creek that gave the
area its name was nearby, so there was little
chance of the fire spreading. Nancy hoped that
the ploy would give her the time she needed to
spirit her father away.

Nancy hurried across the open area and
checked the inside of the shed. There was little
of value that she could see. Some wood was
stacked on one side, some empty boxes sat on
the other; in between there were a few shovels

and hoses, a couple of empty burlap bags, and a lot of dust and dirt.

Gritting her teeth, Nancy lit a match and put it on the burlap bag. It caught at once and spread quickly to the boxes and wood. Nancy backed out of the shed and ran to the lodge. Pounding on the door, she began shouting, "Fire! Help! Fire!"

The man she'd seen with her father came running, his face dark with anger. "What in the world are you doing out here, girl?" he demanded when he opened the door.

"I was driving by and I saw smoke," Nancy told him. "Your shed is on fire." She pointed to where the flames were now licking merrily at the structure.

The man muttered something gruff and pushed her out of the way as he ran toward the shed. Nancy didn't hesitate a moment. She raced inside, through the handsome rooms, and back out the rear door to where her father was still sitting at the table.

"Come on, Dad," she called. "We have to run now."

"Nancy?" He blinked at her owlishly.

"Where on earth did you come from?"

"I'll tell you later," Nancy promised, grabbing his arm and pulling him to his feet. "Come on, we have to hurry."

"I didn't know you were here." He sounded sleepy, but he followed her obediently, stopping only once to look back at the man who was busily spraying the fire with a garden hose. "Shouldn't we help?" he asked.

"Not this time," Nancy answered grimly, dragging him toward her concealed car. Only when they reached it did she feel safe. Still, she didn't waste any time getting her father into the car and driving away from the lodge.

Her father fell asleep before they left the lodge property and slept till they entered the outskirts of Calgary. When he woke, he sat up slowly and looked around, then smiled with a little of his old sparkle.

"So it wasn't a dream," he said, his speech much clearer now. "I was almost afraid to open my eyes."

"What happened, Dad?" Nancy asked.

"I walked into a trap, it was that simple. The man met me at the lodge with a gun. He kept me locked up for several days. Until you called, actually. He was listening to our conversation when I talked to you."

"I thought it was very strange," Nancy admitted.

"Then he made me write a couple of crazy letters to Hannah. That's all I remember. After that he started giving me some sleeping pills and . . ." He shrugged. "Then I looked up and you were there. Do you have any idea what is going on?"

"I sure do," Nancy told him, her heart light now that she knew he was going to be all right. "I'll tell you the whole story as soon as we get a place to stay for the night and make some plane reservations for tomorrow. And I have some phone calls to make, too. There are a lot of people worrying about you, you know."

Food and rest were somewhat neglected during the next twelve hours as Nancy contacted Ned and Grace, then Hannah, reassuring them and making arrangements for their flight back to River Heights. She also told her father the entire story, then listened as he called the proper authorities to arrange for the arrest of the man at Chain Creek Lodge and for the apprehension of Barry and Fred Mathews in Cheyenne.

His final call the next morning was to River Heights and after he hung up the receiver, he turned to Nancy with a smile. "Well, super-sleuth," he said, "you've really achieved a miracle this time."

"What do you mean?" Nancy asked.

"We've just been invited to the Winthrop mansion for a family reunion party—a reunion that you made possible."

"Then Mr. Winthrop is feeling better?" Nancy asked. "Hannah said that he'd been very ill."

"Seems that having his daughter and her family taking care of him has changed things considerably, or maybe it's the result of *not* having Tom and Madge Mathews in charge of things." Her father looked grim. "It seems that Tom was the mastermind behind everything—along with his brother, of course, who dreamed up the idea of keeping me a prisoner at the lodge. Tom confessed the moment he came face-to-face with Clarinda and Lorna."

"All because he didn't want Clarinda to inherit?" Nancy asked.

"Obviously he wanted the money for himself," her father replied. "He's been in charge of Mr. Winthrop's affairs for quite a few years, and I suspect he may have been taking small sums of money from the man's accounts. Winthrop didn't notice, but over the years it probably added up to quite a bit. I'm sure Mathews has been afraid to have the records examined. Well, whatever the reason, he's going to be spending the next few months answering a lot of questions and I doubt any of them will be pleasant."

"The party will be, though," Nancy said. "I'm really looking forward to meeting Clarinda Winthrop in person."

"I'm just looking forward to going home with my brave and brilliant daughter," her father told her, putting his arm around her shoulders. "I'm very proud of you, Nancy, and very glad that I asked you to help me with this case."

As he spoke, he had no idea that another one was already brewing for Nancy when she faced the *Clue in the Ancient Disguise.*

"I'm glad you asked me, too," Nancy said with a grin. "The rodeo was loads of fun."

NANCY DREW MYSTERY STORIES®
by Carolyn Keene

The Triple Hoax (#57)
The Flying Saucer Mystery (#58)
The Secret in the Old Lace (#59)
The Greek Symbol Mystery (#60)
The Swami's Ring (#61)
The Kachina Doll Mystery (#62)
The Twin Dilemma (#63)
Captive Witness (#64)
Mystery of the Winged Lion (#65)
Race Against Time (#66)
The Sinister Omen (#67)
The Elusive Heiress (#68)

You will also enjoy
THE LINDA CRAIG™ SERIES
by Ann Sheldon

The Palomino Mystery (#1)
The Clue on the Desert Trail (#2)
The Secret of Rancho del Sol (#3)
The Mystery of Horseshoe Canyon (#4)
The Mystery in Mexico (#5)
The Ghost Town Treasure (#6)